[The 28 Mansions

A novel by

[MOTAZ H MATAR]

Copyright Registration Service
Ref: 7812054863

MOTAZ H MATAR © 2019

A letter from Ibn Arabi to the reader:

I saw El-Khizr three times in my life, once I saw him in Seville, and another time in Fezz, the last time I saw him was in Al-Mosul. Every time I saw him – he would hand me his cloak, like he was gifting it to me, as if I'm about to be someone special, unique, and different. And here it goes, I come back after 852 years, with my cloak to gift it to someone, someone who would understand spiritual elevation. When I look around me, I see the world dissonant, opposed and the trials has lit up a fire in every corner of the world as if the world is about to come to an end. I decided to come back, and now I cannot go back. I came back to see Al-Andalus different from the Al-Andalus I used to know and a Seville different from the Seville I knew. What has occurred to mankind? Will my visions and dreams help humanity's affliction? Maybe there's a chance that someone might read my letters – and maybe - just maybe - make a difference in himself, and the world.

"I owe an endless debt to love, therefore I have
ridden its waves:
Love is my religion and faith." – Ibn Arabi

Prelude:

"I killed her. I killed her!" Yassin screamed with a voice that shattered the silence of the night.

Yassin wrote in his journal: "It was this night that I came back to life, the night I came back to the place which I loved the most: Seville. The place where my dreams became one with death, and life was overcome with tears and hope to reunite again with the one I loved the most, the person I dreamed of the most, and with the worst fears I had of a life that is no longer worth living."

I saw the Great Master, Ibn Arabi, hundreds of times in my imagination, in my mind, and in my sleep and he told me his story about when he was young and met El-Khizr, the master of absolute wisdom, the master of knowledge, and the teacher of Moses:

"My son, shall I lead you to the Ultimate Tree of the Universe?" El-Khizr asked him. "For if you find it, you will find your complete self." El-Khizr paused, then continued. "You have to travel to the ends of the world, looking for the tree just like you look for your loved one. Go to Seville; there you will find the Ultimate Tree."

"There you will find what you have been looking for all your life. But be careful, you have to cross the long roads and bear the hardships. You will find four birds: the Ringdove, the Royal Eagle, the Jet-Black Crow, and at last you will meet the Phoenix.

Then you will know that you are coming close to the Ultimate Tree of the Universe."

El-Khizr looked at the sky filled with stars, then he gazed towards the moon, leaving the young Ibn Arabi in both in wonder and disillusionment.

Part One

The Ringdove: The Soul

"I am the ringdove of beginnings; my
dwelling is the Garden of spirituality.
I am an eye amongst witnesses, I have no
place but those beginnings."

*--Ibn Arabi, The Discourse of the Ringdove, The
Universal Tree and the four birds.*

Chapter 1: Alif

Awaken me from the vision that took me by storm. Awaken me from the dream where I spoke gracefully for the first time.

Ask the dream that opened up to the world like a window.

Ask it about the suffering and the sudden unexpected arrival that it has on us like a shooting star falling from nowhere with the speed of light.

Ask the dream one more time why I was born without the ability to roll my tongue and communicate with the world. Why have I, Yassin, never spoken a word?

Ask it about the childhood, the smell of garden flowers, and bicycle rubber screeching on the pavement of the street. Ask it about the sense of touch, the smell, and the hearing. Ask the dream about the first registered memory, and the first frame.

Acknowledge the fact that I always wanted to see the world through wide-open doors and not through tiny windows. I have asked myself hundreds of times: did I really want to die? Did I want to jump from my apartment's balcony and end it all? It may be that I felt helpless, or even careless. It may have been the fear I had of hitting the ground, thinking of how painful it would be, and how horrible it would make me feel.

"Am I a bird that loves to fly?" I would sit on the edge of the balcony and imagine that I had wings, close my eyes and let myself be at one with the horizon and the void overcoming it all.

Ahead of me was the day which I have been waiting for all my life. My first day to work at the Museum of Seville. I was surprised that my query letter actually received a reply. I accepted the job and hoped for the best. "A clerk?" I thought to myself. Sounds dull. The basement room where I sat to translate, the piles of papers, the ceiling clustered, running and smelly pipes. To the side of my desk, was a small window to the street. Like a cat, looking at people's walking feet, I wondered how the time passed by and yet at the same time how the university days felt like a day or two. Maybe because I spent most of my college days looking at piles of papers and reading about the history of Al-Andalus in the times of the Moors. Art? Music? Science? Every time, the colors of the city would change when I remembered the Moorish Andalusia. It was as if I had recalled the Moorish Kings and Queens, and asked life to bring me back there. Then I would settle into reality again and realize that I was only a lonesome student sitting in his dorm room looking at the world with glaring eyes.

As I entered the Museum on the first day, it looked like something from a fairytale. Long stairs lead to the main hall. There were millions of books in the library, and the gallery hall was filled with Andalusian paintings which hung from the walls like they were stars aligned in the widespread sky. "My God!" I said to myself. "It felt like I have stepped into a heaven with no vanishing point."

And then she came around the corner. She stood like a respected queen. Mira was her name, it was written on her office's door. Maybe she truly was a Moorish queen. She was the most beautiful person I had ever seen in my entire life. I was scared that the bright light coming from her side would blindfold me and I would become blind. She looked not only like she owned the space, but all of Andalusia.

At that moment, our eyes met. "Please speak to me. Speak with the language of the beating heart that is intertwined with excitement and fear. Please tell me that what I am experiencing here is real!" I thought to myself, overcome by her beauty.

She crossed the room. "So, you are real," she finally said, and then laughed.

"I thought you were never going to come. I am really happy you are here. Let's meet at five o'clock, and I will tell you what I need from you. By the way, you're welcome."

***

All day long, I wondered if she knew that I could not iterate any words, that I was a mute. I'm sure she knew, or did she? Churning these thoughts, I noticed a sign outside the entrance to the museum which I haven't before. The sign was designed with beautiful Arabic calligraphy. It said: The opening of the chamber of the Andalusian Mystic *"Ibn Arabi"* in the Museum of Seville on the 28th of February.

It was the first day of February.

Afternoon sped by, and thus came evening. A cup of coffee sat on the cafeteria's table. The steam from the cup passed the time. I lit a cigarette, and then another. The smoke from my cigarette formed circles then a cloud which then began shaping into different faces, faces that frowned, and some that smiled. I thought I saw Mira's face in the smoke. She welcomed me with a smile, and said: "Are you free this evening?"

And then shockingly, I was taken back to the Museum, and saw her in front of me. "Did you read the sign at the door?" She said as she loudly dropped a pile of papers on my desk. "Can you translate the Arabic text inside these letters by tomorrow morning? We need to hurry. We only have 28 days until the opening."

Then she walked out of the cafeteria and got into her car like she was never here. Everything

10

looked so dull after she left. I took a big last gulp of coffee and hurried back inside Museum to start working.

Among the piles of paper which Mira had given me was a journal. A worn dark brown leather journal that had the title "Ibn Arabi" inscribed on it with Arabic font. I eagerly opened it. It was dated with the year 1190. At the bottom of the front page, I read the words: "Seville, Al-Andalus".

I skimmed through the Journal and started reading it.

Adam: Divine Wisdom

The youngster deeply indulged in visions. To him they felt like dreams, dreams in which he was searching for his hometown, for love that he had lost all his life. This is when he saw El-Khizr with his white beard standing by the sea, looking into the waves, indulged. The youngster walked a few steps towards him and then stopped. The old man felt that the youngster was coming his way like he had a revelation from the sky.

"Meet me where the two seas meet, I will show you where to find your Nizam."

The youngster woke up from his dreams shaking and shivering. He woke up to a quiet night, but he still felt scared. The night frightened him and made him feel lonelier. He tried to go back to sleep, but his eyes wouldn't shut.

"Was the Master El-Khizr here, or was I just dreaming?" he said to himself.

"Did he leave the window open before he fell asleep?" The youngster asked himself this while he waited for the sun to rise before he could walk to the sea. He felt saddened for leaving his home but decided to go anyway.

The beams of light sent serenity to the world. When he arrived at the sea, he saw El-Khizr standing there with his white cloak, and his white beard.

"I will tell you where to find your Nizam. I'll take you to her."

The youngster remained astonished while listening to El-Khizr speak. Silence prevailed for a few seconds.

"To find your Nizam, you have to find the four birds," El-Khizr said. When you meet them you will find your Nizam. You will find the adoration you are looking for."

The youngster was hesitant. Something deep inside of him filled him with joy for he knew that he was on his way to Nizam. What the youngster didn't know was that the road was going to be rough, full of hardships, but nevertheless, he was curious, and he wanted to explore the journey that El-Khizr prophesized.

The youngster travelled in his mystical journey to search for the meaning of humanity. To search for Nizam, and for the meaning of dreams. The youngster sailed with El-Khizr on a small boat crossing the sea, away from Seville, away from his beloved home, away from childhood's dreams, hoping to find the four birds and the universal tree.

"What are the four birds?" the youngster asked.

El-Khizr responded: "Wait until you see with your own eyes. Wait until you see the ultimate truth. Go learn my son, that in your journey, you will be searching for the perfect human: for Adam and all the names. Go learn, my son, that in your journey you will be looking for the perfect human, you will be looking for all the names of the Divine, and for the Ultimate Tree of the Universe."

"Take the wisdom from Adam's story. Would you turn away from it and walk away? Would you live to learn from it, or would you forget? Would you ditch the lessons given to you and neglect? Go and learn my son that in your mystical journey, you will be looking for the Universe, for the reason of your existence, for your journey in this life, for your birth, and for your death."

"What is wisdom?" The youngster asked.

"My son, you must first ask yourself what the Divine wisdom is. Look at you, look at man and the story of creation, look at the blessing you were granted: the blessing to be in the world. The blessing to become alive from a single piece of clay."

"Beware, my son, of the Adam within you, for he is fragile and weak, loving but sinful. My son, you are yourself a realm of contradictions and miracles. Inside of you is love and hatred, beauty and vile, fear and courage, betrayal and faithfulness. You are a mirror for the universe with all contrasts and wonders, with its colors and manifestations. My son beware of the first sin, and the first fall. Beware of the Tree and don't make it a choice."

El-Khizr paused and then continued. "If you do make that choice, you will leave your paradise that was designed for you with greens and trees, with running waters and streams, full of miracles and wonders, you will return to earth, your mortal home."

"My son, do I lead you to the ultimate wealth and immortality? Hear those whispers in the ears of Adam. Look at the world around you and ponder your thoughts. Think of the reason of telling. Think of killing and blood shedding. Think of man's struggles and obsessions. Think of his tribulations and endless finite desires. Think of those ones that scatter like the sand slipping away from your hand, and those which vanish like a lake which has fully dried out."

"My son, you are about to embark on a journey of discovery, and I will tell you this: Find yourself in it and find your love: don't be afraid to love. Search for yourself in it and be it. One day you will wake up and hear the calling: the calling of the Divine wisdom.

Chapter 2: Ba

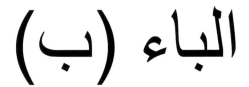

Because behind those hidden walls, there was evil.

Because **B**ader's name started with the letter "Ba", the second letter of the Alphabet. Both of us born twins.

Between those split seconds, we were separated.

Beneath it all, beneath the hidden treasure lay so many secrets of the world, and so many realities.

"Do you know that you have a precious gem in your hands? That you have access to the most expensive treasure in Spain?" Bader asked me.

"**B**rother, instead of landing that stupid job of yours, you could've been a Moorish King," said Bader, interrupting his speech because he didn't want the waiter to hear the conversation, he continued. "You must claim it back."

He took a leaflet from his pocket and put it in front of me. It was a leaflet from the Museum of Seville.

I took the leaflet and read what was written on it:

"The grand opening of the special exhibit: The chamber of Ibn Arabi".

Barely able to hide my disgust, I threw the brochure back at him. I wished that the ground would swallow me.

"I don't think you realize what's inside the chamber," Bader said, leaning forward and locking eyes with me.

Bearing the few moments of silence, he spoke again.

"Brother, it's the most expensive tapestry in the world. It dates back to more than a 1,000 years ago. It's priceless."

***

By God, his words fell down on me like hail. I had to cover my face and protect my ears. His words made me want to vomit. How could I explain to him that I don't want to be part of his plan? How could I explain that the hidden treasure is not the key to his salvation?

Brother! let us become one in our thinking. Brother let us balance the boat of life so that it doesn't sink us. Bader, your name means "full moon", but who said that if you were the moon, you are my brother? Because if I dreamt of a brother, I wouldn't dream of Bader. I would dream of the waning moon instead. I would dream to hide behind a dark curtain like a silhouette figure.

Better? Would I feel better? Would I still dream to become like a feather? Fly away in the high skies and disappear in the ether?

"Brother, I don't want to hear this no more, I don't want to hear any more of your excuses, your stories, your words," but of course, he wouldn't hear me.

I am done becoming your other. All my life, I spent being your shadow. I was always there to protect you from yourself, from your evil other. Did our Mother ever think that you were a Moorish King, but not your other?"

"Brother, Brother." I said those words again, and I headed back to the Museum to translate the letters. The guard welcomed me in when he saw my badge, and I went in.

But then I paused. Between the second letter, and the second beat, I wished I would get lost in the beat of the heart. I saw a sign, I saw a face, I saw Mira; I thought. But the evening was quiet and full of lusting for Mira, lusting for a different kind of desire. The ticking clocks would bring her back, maybe another day. The clock in her office, ticking. The basement, empty as ever. The Museum becoming bare and lonesome. I tried to stop thinking, but, how could I? Why would I? There was a stream of thoughts which I had enjoyed, and another which I despised. Both of them crossed each other like two streets on a highway that intersected. If you stood there you would get swept away to the unknown.

Seth: Divine Inspiration

"Dream my Son", This is what El-Khizr told the youngster when they were in the middle of the sea.

The skies full of stars lit up a world of dreams in El-Khizr's eyes.

"Dream my son; make your dream a reality. In every dream there's a beginning and a hidden life - yet to be lived."

In the middle of the sea, the youngster thought that the night was long, and the journey was endless.

"When will we arrive to the sea shore and to safety?" the youngster asked.

"Go learn, my son, that Seth was saddened for saying goodbye to his father Adam," El-Khizr replied.

"Go learn that before Seth, Cain killed Abel, for Seth to become a force calling for righteousness."

"Dream my son, dream of goodness. Dream of the journey ahead of you."

The journey continued until the boat got closer to the shore. The youngster could see the shoreline.

"I can see the shoreline!" the youngster exclaimed with enthusiasm.

But it was too late, water was filling the small boat and it was about to sink.

"My son, through the divine inspiration, you will find the many meanings of the Divine, and the comprehensive unity of all the names. He is the rescuer, and protector. He's your guide in times of danger and fear. He's your guide in times of confusion and disarray."

Despite the youngster's nervousness, El-Khizr was serene and tranquil.

With every passing minute, the boat was sinking deeper in the water until the youngster thought that they were going to die.

"Will we die? Will the water suck us in?"

The youngster screamed again, and his voice echoed in the horizon.

"Swim until you reach the shore line," El-Khizr told the youngster.

The youngster found himself swimming, flapping his arms like a fish moves her fins. The youngster closed his eyes and swam.

Few moments later, he found himself lying on the seashore next to El-Khizr. The youngster thanked the Divine and prayed. Prayed that he was saved, prayed that he was given a second chance to live.

Chapter 3: Ta

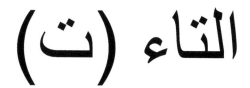

التاء (ت)

Take me to the priceless tapestry only two floors above my head. The tapestry, like a love out of reach, like Mira's marble irises, like the merging of the sun and the rain.

To come back to reality again. To the boring reality, to the place where we get sick sometimes, and others feel sad. Where we get bored with ourselves and wish to peel off our own skin.

Today, not tomorrow. I want everything unhappened. Maybe I could escape and jump on the nearest train, taking me to a different journey, and to a better tomorrow.

To dream Mira into life. Whenever I called her name, I would wake up from a dream into another, and her voice would fade in like a magical tune.

"I think this is fantastic, magical", Mira said.

She paused as she gave me more papers to translate.

"Could you please translate the rest of the letters?"

I was happy that she liked the translations. I nodded my head and took the papers from her.

"Can you finish them by tomorrow morning?"

Talk to her, tell her everything you are thinking of. I nodded my head. And I did what I could do best: glance. And there, she was already gone. Just like in life, where beautiful moments vanish in a second, and things that ache feel like they stay with us a whole lifetime. Every time she came down the stairs it felt like a breath of fresh air coming at me, like someone has opened a window, and let the pure breeze of spring arrive once and for all.

Tear the loud noise and indulge in silence. There passed some moments and I closed my eyes indulging in silence. Then I read the next batch of papers which Mira had handed me. I thought about if I should go back to Bader and nod my head instead.

"That, I'll take as a yes," he said when we were sitting in the old café downtown. Did I nod my head or gesture instead? That, I won't confuse with a gesture, a yes is a big yes, and a no is a no. "Do you know?" I asked myself. "Do you know that you are a brother to an evil brother? You know better than to run away and disappear, vanish from the world if you can."

Thank you, brother, for everything, every word, and every speech you gave me. Thank you for the reality which you made unfold before my eyes. That of which I now call "Brotherhood," that of which occurs because of the blood we share running in our veins.

22

"Thank you," he said.

"I know you will not fail me," but he meant to say: "I know that you will do what everything I say, and you will follow me all the way."

Sometimes we become slaves to those we love, who claim to adore us, and are willing to die with us and for us. Maybe the truth is that they are willing to live and leave us to die. We can at least try to accept them, humor them and travel with them till the end of the line, wondering if it will hurt us, or fall like hammer on our heads and break it into small shattered pieces?

Noah (Most glorified)

My son! Go learn that the Divine has glorified himself above everything: Above the skies, the oceans, and the earth.

My son! To find your way, you have to be close to earth: Be like the soil, the water, and the wind. My son be like the sun. Have a shining light but be humble. If your light fades away, people will miss the sunlight and the warmth.

Be like Noah when he was building his Ark, in the stark daylight, in the hard weather, and the dark.

Whenever the chiefs of his people passed by him, they mocked him. "Construct the Ark within my sight and under my guidance," The Divine told Noah. "Then when the command comes, and the fountains of the Earth gush forth, take on board pairs of every species, male and female, and your people except those of them against whom the Word has already been issued: and address me not in respect of those who are unjust; for verily they shall be drowned in the flood."

Unwavering is the patience that Noah beheld. "My son! Don't be frightened if the people mock you. Look in their eyes and smile, and head on constructing your ark."

"Go learn, my son, that pride is your nemesis. With pride, your strengths will wither away, your faith will shatter, and you will remain looking for your adoration in the ether."

"There is no eternal existence after all except for the eternal force, except for the glorious, for the most glorified."

The youngster remained in deep silence, for several seconds, listening to El-Khizr and pondering these thoughts.

El-Khizr stopped his travelling when he saw a hovel.

"Go my Son, knock, and ask in the hovel if we can be their guests for tonight…"

"How would we be guests for people we never met before?" The youngster asked.

"There in this hovel lives a beautiful, good hearted woman. Her name is Yamama. Go and ask her if we can be her guests for tonight. She will not let us down, I am certain."

The youngster asked no questions. He went ahead and knocked on the door and waited.

Chapter 4: Tha

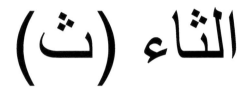

Some **th**ings come and go into our life, and some things that come never fade away. Mira entered the "Chamber of Ibn Arabi" thinking about the words which Yassin had translated. She felt dazed.

"Is there a connection between the words and the Tapestry?" she thought to herself.

There, she looked at the Tapestry, feeling as if she was transcending into another universe.

"**Th**ink", she said under her breath. "Think of the Tapestry's hidden secret," she repeated to herself, and when she was done, she said to herself: "Think again, may you unveil a hidden treasure one day."

Thoroughly she invested in her thoughts. "What does the embroidered image mean? Who created it? When? How? And Why? If we unlock its secret, would we unlock the secret of the universe? The secret to the world in which we are living in?"

The Tapestry shone in the chamber like a full moon in the sky. If you looked at it from an angle, it looked like it consisted of different phases of the moon. Once, it would look like a full moon, and another time, it would look like a waxing moon. If you blinked, the moon would become a waning moon, and then again would become a new moon.

Thematically, Mira noticed that the Tapestry had 28 orbits. In each orbit, there was a moon woven, and in each moon, there were engraved letters of the Arabic Alphabets. Every moon seemed connected and aligned just like a sky full of stars. Mira remembered the day of her event: it was also on the 28th of February. Everything seemed to make sense at certain times, but some other times it didn't. Was she overthinking it, or was it all inter-connected and part of a master plan?

Thwarting fate is not possible, but she tried anyway. "Was it all a coincidence?" She asked herself. Although Mira didn't believe in a force that existed in the Universe, something deep inside her was changing. Every time she would enter the chamber, she would lose herself in the process: time would freeze, and she would feel that she was at one with the universe.

Thousands and thousands of unresolved riddles were floating in the horizon when Mira opened the door of her apartment. She wanted to write her father a letter to tell him a lot of things: how she felt, what she experienced, and what was going on inside of her mind. She couldn't find the words to explain all of these things. She was happy to send him the translated texts of Ibn

Arabi's letters as they were. Mira was not good at interpreting her own thoughts, she believed in facts that had closed ends to them. As she put herself to sleep, she couldn't wait for the next sun to rise so she would see what it had in store for her.

***

Thunder and storms hit us hard that night until I thought that the end was inevitable. It was like the sky was raging, trying to tell me something. How could anyone think in his mind that glory will last, and joy could be replaced with money and power? I wondered what the Tapestry would tell Bader if it could speak. Would it hate the wall that she'll be hanging on? Or the vendor who would set his dirty fingers on it? Would she mock Bader? Would she allow herself to be sold in an auction market and be replaced with paper money? But it seemed that Bader had something planned.

"I have a plan," Bader said as he was smoking another cigarette. He was sitting on the edge of the balcony pretending not to be afraid to die.

"You know why I am not afraid to fall?" he asked, and then added. "You will not fail when you know that you are doing the right thing, with seventy thousand wives waiting for you."

Thankfully, you didn't let go of your will to fall. Hang on tight brother, for at any moment you might slip and fall, and then you will hit your head hard, and that pain would be impossible to bare.

"I want you to get the access code for the Ibn Arabi Chamber," he said to me while looking at me with savage eyes.

Theatre curtains opening, lights fading out. Bader stepped down from the edge of the balcony and walked closer to me, putting his hands on my shoulders. He was still looking me in the eye. I felt I had nowhere else to go. I just wanted to hide from him, escape, or maybe disappear and not see his face again.

"On the 28th of February, you will walk out of the Museum carrying the Tapestry. And then go back inside as if nothing happened. Nobody will doubt a mute moor who works in the basement."

There was a moment of silence. A silence that felt so loud, painful and piercing.

I wished to thaw my heart after the breaking silence. A coldness had set in between the both of us: strange and ironic. Maybe it was the fog coming from my breath, and the cold weather becoming even colder.

"That day will come, and everyone will be busy. Your job will be finished as a clerk. You will disappear from the Museum and from the face of the earth and start a new life."

Thinking it over and over again made my soul ache, made me feel like I was a prisoner of brotherhood. Like a prisoner who was living in his cell.

A cell that was like a hole from hell. I wanted to leave, but I was stuck there for eternity: a doomed eternity.

Idris (The Most Holy)

إدريس

The youngster stood in front of the most beautiful woman in the Universe. He couldn't speak. His eyes were lost staring at the most beautiful eyes he'd ever seen, endlessly.

He asked Yamama if he and his Master could stay for the night.

"I'm sorry. I'm a lonely woman here. I cannot have a young man like you and his old man over," she said.

"It's a cold night, and we don't have food or shelter."

Yamama felt sorry for the youngster, and after a few seconds of silence, she said: "I have a place which has a tiny room behind my hovel. You can stay in it for one night till the morning light comes, and a new day shines in the horizon. I have food for you and your old man that will only be enough for one night."

The youngster felt a relief of joy. His heart was flattered. He thanked Yamama for her offering.

El-Khizr said to the youngster: "Thank the Divine for the blessing of having a shelter and food which he has given you. Thank him for the

31

air which you breathe, the food you eat, and the water which you drink. With faith, you can achieve a lot of your desired wishes. Seek knowledge, for Idris was the father of philosophers. He was the first prophet to be guided by the stars and see the light of the Divine. Through the stars he fumbled the eternal question."

"What is the eternal question?" the youngster asked.

"The eternal question of when and how, the eternal question of the truth." El-Khizr answered.

"What is the truth, my Master?" the youngster asked again.

"The truth of the eternal force that exists in the universe. The one that makes you see. The one that wakes you up in the morning and puts you to sleep at night; the one that makes you want to seek knowledge. What is the Universe we live in, and how do we understand it? Aren't these the two questions that irritated mankind forever? These two questions will help you when you reiterate your thoughts and think again of the world around you."

"Write your thoughts, my son. Write everything that comes to your mind. Maybe a day will come where your writings will reach the end of the world, and people will read your written words. Adorn every second of your time, for truly time can be snatched away just in a second. Just like life can be snatched away, in a flash of light."

El-Khizr was transcended, looking at the stars in the deep sky.

"The sky tonight is full of stars. The stars float like a ship floats on the surface of the ocean".

"Are you a poet?"

The youngster heard a voice. It was Yamama, and she was standing behind him.

"No. I am not."

"But your words are beautiful." Yamama said.

When the youngster looked at Yamama again, he had a sigh of relief like a newborn coming to life.

Yamama's hand landed on the youngster's shoulder, his heart jumped from its place.

"Where do you come from?" asked Yamama.

"I come from Seville, but I have travelled away from it."

"Oh, are you from beautiful Seville?"

"Yes, but I don't know if I will ever go back to it because I embarked on a journey."

"Where are you destined to go?"

"I am heading to where I will find love, hoping that I will find joy, inner-peace, and love."

"Love? What are you looking for in love?"

"I am looking for a love where the heart will settle, where the heart will feel like it has found home."

"Do you think that the heart will ever find its eternal home?"

"If I knew the answer, I wouldn't be here…"

The youngster and Yamama spent the night contemplating the universal questions of life, love, and wisdom.

The long hours of the night passed by. The youngster wasn't aware of the night which passed by so quickly. He realized that the sun was about to rise and was getting ready to get back to his travels.

When the youngster went to see El-Khizr he found him prostrating with serenity. The youngster waited for El-Khizr to finish his prayers to tell him that the sun was about to rise and that they had to continue with their journey.

"Did you wake him up?"

"He's deeply invested in his deep prayers."

Yamama paused before she uttered these words.

"Will you ever come back here?"

"One day, I might. My destiny might bring me back here. What is the reason for you asking?"

"I have a feeling that you will be back here, but..."

Their speech was interrupted by the presence of El-Khizr.

"Are you ready my Master?"

The youngster and his Khizr thanked Yamama for her warm hospitality and went on to continue the next part of their journey.

Chapter 5: Jeem

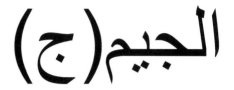

Just as I went back to the Museum that afternoon, I had a feeling like I was going out of breath, sinking deeper into the water, knowing I had a few days, maybe hours, before I run out of oxygen.

Jogging in an endless street, looking at the silhouette figure ahead of me. An irrepressible feeling struck, an explicitness of trying to reach the person standing far away from me like a mirage. Every time I approached the figure, it moved away. Before I even know what was going on, I found myself falling into a deep sleep. All I could remember is a memory of a dream like déjà vu. It felt like a dream I had experienced before. I suddenly opened my eyes, and there she was. It was Mira standing in front of me with her hands on my shoulders, trying to wake me up.

"Wake up, wake up, it's five o'clock," she said.

I Jumped out of my chair and slowly opened my eyes and looked in her direction. I felt like her eyes could speak to me. I was frozen in my chair.

"Do you have the translated letters?" Mira asked me.

I handed her the papers, and as usual, she left.

I joined forces with torture in this world. I learned that there are two types of torture in this world: The sweet torture and the bitter one. Which one is more painful? Which one is worse on the victim? The one that leaves a permanent scar like a tattoo on his body till the day he dies, or the one that fades away but leaves you lost in your thoughts like a mad man?

Joyfully, I wondered this as I walked back home in the streets of Seville. I walked for so long that I had no desire for the walk to the end. I walked, and I felt that I passed by all the people that ever lived. I felt that Seville was at the center of the universe. That Seville was the beginning and the end. I felt for the first time, that humanity began here, and would end here. I wondered why I was having these thoughts: I would twist between joyous feeling and hollow ones, sweet and sour, nostalgic and apathetic.

Juxtaposed were two images that I saw as I walked on the narrow streets of Seville. One of love, and the other of restlessness. When I would think of Mira, I imagined that she was with me during my walks and I would tell her of everything that crossed my mind in that moment.

Jabbed by those never-ending thoughts, I would tell her the things that I loved and the things that I hated. I would tell her about my strengths and weaknesses, my dreams and nightmares. I imagined that I would tell her of my favorite moments in life, and lowest points. I would laugh with her and then cry. I would take her hand and run or jump from a cliff into the cold water of the ocean – hoping that the water would not freeze us, and I would still be alive to come back to her and live the whole experience with her, over and over again.

Jaded after all these thoughts, all I wanted was a resting shore. But that never came. In a flash, I stood on the side of the road, and thought I saw a ghost: I saw Bader standing at the side of the road, looking me in the eye.

Abraham (Ecstatic Love)

إبراهيم

El-Khizr and the youngster went along in their journey. In the middle of the desert El-Khizr sat and built a fire, so they would find some warmth.

"Let me share with you the story of Prophet Abraham. Think of hardships, think of fire. And then ask yourself: Would your body tolerate the heat? Think then of fire turning into water. Think of heat turning into cold. Think of the words of the Divine: We said: O fire! Be a comfort and peace to Ibrahim.

The fire is destined to burn you, and the water is destined to drown you, but it could also have mercy on you. There's not a single road that is free of hardships and horrors. There's no spring without winter. Look at the sky, you will see it is full of stars, but look again you will see a clear sky, clear enough to heal your wounds and purify your heart.

Look at these far away mountains. 'Have you not believed' the Divine told Abraham, 'Yes, but I ask only that my heart may be reassured.'

'Take four birds and commit them to yourself. Then after slaughtering them put on each hill a portion of them; then call them - they will come [flying] to you in haste. And know that the Lord is Exalted in Might and Wise.'

Who amongst us doesn't want reassurance for his heart?"

"How is the heart reassured?" asked the youngster.

"The heart is never reassured my son, but it is always looking for reassurance. For it is always torn, lost, looking for its own resting place. There's no escape, for your heart has an address: An eternal adoration, and pure conscience. In it, the heart knows itself, and finds its reflection. In it, the heart finds its friends, its childhood dreams, and its youth."

"Be like the bird my son, spread your wings, and don't be afraid to fall down, for you must fall, time, and time, and time again. You will weep hundreds of times in your life time, but don't lose hope.

"Fly my son! Fly, but don't forget to land on earth, and tread."

"Think of Hajar, Abraham's wife. Think of her travels and journeys and the well of Zamzam."

"What is Zamzam"? The youngster asked.

"In the well of Zamzam, you will find the symbol of motherhood, and the fountain of life.

Even if the desert dried out before your eyes. Hit the ground with your stick, and it will grant you a well of endless water."

Chapter 6: Hha

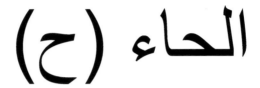

H'aram means Forbidden. Has adoration become forbidden? How does the heart know that it has fallen in love? How does it know that it has become weak and helpless? How does it know that its paths are endless?

Had I not been restless all day, I could've faced my Brother and put an end to this feeling that I was a slave of his. But on that day Mira asked me to accompany her.

The way upstairs seemed so far, the way to chamber seemed like it was a pathway to heaven. Mira entered the pin code on the door of the Chamber. Part of me wanted to see the code of the Chamber. Because when you try not to think of evil, you can't help but think of it. Maybe because Bader's thoughts were overcoming me, attacking me, and penetrating me. It's like his words have become my thoughts, and I have embraced everything about him: The way he thinks and the way he talks.

Mira opened the door, and we went inside the "Chamber of Ibn Arabi."

Hold on. Hold your strengths together. I was shaking, as I was waiting for Mira to uncover the most precious and the oldest Andalusian treasure to date. I took a few more steps inside, coming closer to the Tapestry which was covered with a white cloth. I looked around me, and all the walls were white, everything was white, all dressed in white. There was a dimmed light pointed on the Tapestry that was hanging there. Mira turned to me.

"Are you ready?" She asked.

Here, my heart started beating fast. Like someone struck by lightning. I froze. As she removed the white cloth, my brain was raced a million thoughts a second.

"There it is, there is the Tapestry!" Mira said quietly.

I stood there looking at the Tapestry as if time had just swallowed me into a black hole.

Had I ever seen something more beautiful in my entire life? I don't remember seeing the moon as stunning as I have seen it then. It was there attached to its 28 orbits, each orbit bringing its own wonder to the Tapestry like each one of the orbits was a day full of joy, beauty, and love.

***

Help me heal your pain and wounds, I sat there as I was looking at her typing something on her computer. Did Mira have a father? Does someone like Mira have a father? Was she ever born? How does the world give birth to angels?

41

Does the Universe spark with light? Or does the sun shy away from their light?

Hear my footsteps walking back, but all I could remember was that I had leaped down the stairs to the basement, and back to the office. I was immersed. It was like time was being compressed into fractions of seconds: like the moment we are born or the moment in which we depart from this world.

Hovering over me like an angel, I saw Mira looking at me from over her desk. I continued writing. Mira was sitting next to me, looking at me as I was writing. I couldn't look her straight in the eye. I shied away.

Her words fell like thunder and a soft breeze. "I am just enjoying looking at you while you work."

"Hey, who are you?" She asked me a little while later, in a soft voice. I thought I saw the beam of light shining from her eyes. I heard those words like a whisper, like a soft wind that blew, penetrating the silence.

One more time, I was out of words. And I was out of time. My words were drying out, like there was no more ink in this world, only a few more drops.

High minded I was and remained, Mira finished me off with a question:

"I think we are like minded. Would you like going out with me for a cup of coffee later this evening?" Mira asked.

Hallucinating, I had no choice but sign my own death sentence: I had no choice but to say yes.

Isaac: Truth

اسحق

The youngster and El-Khizr crossed the desert. They passed by a herd of sheep. El-Khizr told the youngster to count the sheep. When he did, he discovered that they were 99 sheep.

"What happened to the 100th sheep, and where is the Shepard"? The youngster asked.

"I could hear the voice of the Shepard saying: I was asleep at night, and the 100th sheep got lost from the herd".

What do we do with the sheep, my master?" The youngster asked.

"Guard them until the Shepard comes back, for you might become the sheep herder."

"What if the Shepard never comes back to his sheep ever?" Asked the youngster.

"My son! Do not wander around looking for what is lost. One day you might wake up with a revelation that changes your being forever. There is not one truth but many, there is not only one story but many. It's only how you see it, and how you live for it."

"Let me tell you more about the truth. What is the ultimate truth? Seek it out in your awakening and in your sleep."

"Learn my son, to look ahead, and see the bright light of the day. A revelation for you might come in different ways. You are not a prophet my son, but to each one of us there is a revelation."

'Praise be to the Divine who hath given me, in my old age, Ishmael and Isaac! Lo! My Lord is indeed the Hearer of Prayer.'

"My son you are a protector of the sheep. You are here in this world for a purpose. You are the seeker for the truth and justice."

"How is justice achieved?"

"It is never fully achieved, but it is always about to occur. My son if one day thieves broke into your house and transgressed, what would you do? If you were expulsed and they burned your implantations, what would you do? Don't panic my son and work to strengthen your arm. Build a seal around your heart, stand strong."

"My son, the road ahead of you is still long, and the desert is still behind us. We must proceed."

Part Two:

The Royal Eagle: The Spirit

"I am the Eagle with the highest status. To me belongs the beauty and the bright staggering light."
--*Ibn Arabi*, *The Discourse of the Royal Eagle,*

The Universal Tree and the four birds.

Chapter 7: Kha

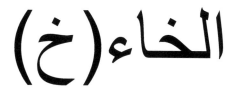

Khaled in Arabic means "Immortal" – the Eternal. That evening was immortal, and it seemed that it was going to last forever. We walked in the old town of Seville. The town was quiet, and the sun was setting on the horizon. We found a bench in the old town's alleys and sat there next to a boutique hotel that looked like it was built in the 16th century.

Khalilati, meant "my best friend". Although we didn't even look into each other's eyes. We both felt utter uneasiness.

"Do you know why I send these emails to my father?" Mira asked me.

She paused for a few seconds, and then she stood up turning her back to me. It was already getting dark as the sun started to set. This was when the rain started drizzling outside. It was cold; and Mira was wearing her coat. It was obvious that she didn't mind the cold weather and the rain.

Mira's words helped bring me back to earth, after I was interrupted by the vision of El-Khizr, once again. The hardest thing was speaking in a language that doesn't exist, and vocalizing sounds in a language that don't exist in another. I felt totally lost and overwhelmed.

"You know, life is …Sometimes, you wonder if things happen for a reason or if everything happens because there is a master plan that determines everything." Mira continued.

I tried to look her in the eye. She was still looking away as if she was mulling what she was going to say.

"How do you feel when you are alive but at the same time gone? How do you feel when you are existing body only, but not soul?"

"Khayal"; Imagination. That was my answer. To imagine is to feel what I feel: being next to you, and with you. I said hoping that she would hear me.

"My father; has lost part of his memory. And I feel like I am losing him slowly, vaguely, and it's …killing me." She said as she looked me in the eye, with her teary eye. "And then you!" She said, then she paused.

"What about me?" the voice inside of me said in a shock.

"Why you?" Mira said. "Why a mute guy like you?"

Mira's tears rolled, she tried to hide it, resist it. I felt sorry for her. But I also felt sorry for myself. I wished that I could break my silence once and for all. Break the cocoon and transform into a butterfly, hoping that I could find my way into the open skies.

"I'm sorry. Forget everything I have said." Mira took the translated letter from a pocket in her coat, and she started reading it.

Ismail: Elevation

اسماعيل

As the youngster and El-Khizr were travelling in their Journey. The youngster listened to the words of El-Khizr.

"Be a guard for the sheep. Be a guard for the visions, and its manifestations, for you might become like prophet Ismail was. When he said to his father: My father, do as you are told. Even when you think you are leading yourself to your demise, what do you do? How do you elevate yourself from existence, and the dream of eternity?"

"My son, who of us doesn't dream to sleep soundly? For each one of us has his visions, and each one of us is a vision. But you are still indifferent from your visions."

"Don't be like the Shepard my son, don't be rest assured, for they are looking at you like you look towards the Divine the merciful. Are you aware of my words my son? When you elevate with your love, you will elevate and come closer to your purpose."

El-Khizr stopped and then said: "We have reached the shop of an old righteous man, who loves the stars. Every night he sits, watches the stars, and counts them. He is a generous old man. My old friend. He will guide us; may he help you on where to find the Nizam. Ask him about the Nizam for he might know, for every tiding has its appointed time. Ask him about love and about your heart which was shattered."

Chapter 8: Dal

Dreamlike! Just like a dream, we were both transformed into another world, and another reality. This time, the words felt so much different, and splendid. Maybe because they were coming out of Mira's mouth. Maybe because our souls were flying over the skies, and landing where they belonged: like birds flapping their wings for eternity.

Day became night, and then the next day came. Like a dancing dervish, I was on my way to the office the next day. I expected Mira to be there early, but she wasn't. I started my work on the letters early that day. I felt so happy and so alive as if I was born again. I found myself contemplating the words Mira had said to me the day before, and her voice: Her voice which was a pathway to heaven and an endless open sky.

I **d**eserved to hear those words from her. Hearing her voice had made up for all the years which I was speechless. I felt like I was regaining my voice – the voice which my soul needed. The voice of true feeling and true emotion. It felt like Mira had given it back to me.

"Sorry about yesterday." I heard her saying as she was coming in one hour later. I didn't mean to say anything to hurt your feelings. I'm sorry."

"**D**on't worry," my smile indicated.

She went back and sat on her desk as if she was trying to avoid me completely. The whole evening passed by, and Mira didn't say anything to me. I started to get worried. Shall I approach her, or should I leave her alone? I was wondering if she was planning to talk to me at all. So, I waited and waited.

Done with my work and translations. It was 5 o'clock. I put the letter on her desk and planned to leave smoothly and swiftly. I didn't want to disturb her after all. I was wondering if we were going to read the letter together. But she didn't bring this up. I left the Museum peacefully – or so I thought.

Down with the ghosts which were chasing me. I was walking home, I thought that I saw my brother standing in front of me like a ghost. But I realized I was only imagining him. It was a frightening moment for I didn't want to see his face. A few moments later I received a text from him.

"Yassin come to my house when you are done. I need to talk to you."

I felt had an urge to face him. What was I going to do this time? How would I tell him that I'm not going to do what he was asking me to do? Maybe this way he'll know that I'm over this once and for all:

YASSIN: Hey Bader, I can't come tonight.
BADER: Are you trying to run away?
YASSIN: No. I'm just afraid.
BADER: What are you scared of?
YASSIN: Of the consequences.
BADER: Are you becoming the coward that I feared you would turn into?
YASSIN: Where are you?
BADER: You know where I am.
YASSIN: Okay, I'm coming your way.

Dangerous, few moments passed by, and I didn't receive any message from Bader. Then my phone beeped. It was a message from Mira.

MIRA: Hey, how are you? I just want to make sure that you are okay. I'm sorry. I hope I didn't make you feel bad. And by the way, thank you for the translations today. I'll read them tonight and tell you what I think. Have a good night. Mira.

My phone beeped again, and it was Bader:

BADER: Where are you?

Damn you, brother! While you knew I was on my way to you. I had hoped that you would forget about me once and for all and forget that I even exist.

****

Decorated with her character and style, Mira sat in her apartment and made herself a cup of tea. She was excited for knowing what the next journey of the youngster and El-Khizr will hold. But first she decided to write her father another email:

Dad, I miss you so much. Sorry I didn't send you anything in the past two days. I was very busy with work. I'm attaching the previous letter which I didn't attach last time. I hope you like it. I am hoping to know what you think of it. I am planning to take some time off work to visit you next week. Can you do me a favor? Can we read the 8th letter together tonight? I'm sending it here within this email. Until we meet again, have a good night. Love you, Mira.

Jacob: Spiritual ease

El-Khizr sat there overcome by sadness. He learnt that his friend who got older, could not be guided by the stars anymore. He went on telling the youngster:

"Thank the Divine who has gifted us with eyes to see. The heart can see further than the eyes can see, and further than the road ahead of us."

The old man is far sighted; his eyesight is supernatural. He would see the stars even when he was a little child. The Divine has granted him a daughter, who can see farther away than him. She would know what is about to happen, and what has occurred. If you were gentle and asked her, she might lead you to your fate: Your fate which is like every new love: pure like rain."

"If you were infected with short eye-sightedness, ask the Divine not to inflict you with the shortness of vision. For the heart sees and the heart hears: If the heart goes blind, then insight will go blind."

"When the heart sees, the Divine will put light in the heart, and the heart will become like a lantern that will light up the way. Your light, my son, is the light of your heart. What has occurred to Prophet Jacob when his eyesight became faint? His love for his son Joseph was enough to give him light both day and night. It was enough to light up his being and his heart."

At that time, the daughter of the old man appeared. It was like when she approached the youngster. She lit up the whole evening with a spark.

"Look at your heart, what does it tell you?" Asked the girl. "Look inside your soul and ask it what it wants from you. Look in your mind, look at your being."

The youngster asked the girl about what her name was.

"My name is Chihana. I am here day and night serving my old man for he is weak and sick."

The girl sensed that the youngster had words in his mouth but was hesitant to speak.

"Can I ask you about something? Maybe you will lead me to it."

"What can I do for you young man?"

"I learned that you were granted far eye sightedness, and I thought that you might be of help to me. I am looking for Nizam. Do you know where and how I can find her?" The youngster asked.

"Each one of us has his own Nizam. You might see her in your sleep, or she might be standing in front of you at a certain moment. You might see her in an evening or maybe in the bright light of day."

"Don't look at her with your eyes but search for her within your own heart. For your heart will find her and recognize her, and your mind will tell you where she resides. You must never get tired from searching. Look for her every morning, and every evening. You might find her in your morning coffee, or your cup of tea, until you know that she is her. She surely will be waiting for you and will recognize you. She will miss you like you miss her. Your soul will adore her, like she adores you."

Chapter 9: Thal

That which I call coincidence, that which I call luck. Fear crawled inside of me like the devil crawls into our chests.

There he was standing on the side of the road; I didn't recognize him at first glance. He was wearing sunglasses at night to hide his eyes, a hood covering his head, and hiding his features.

"Why don't you answer me when I try to contact you?"

The time was almost midnight. Bader spoke again.

"Do you **th**ink that you were going to run away from me"?

He laughed ridiculing me, then walked closer to me and said in a lowered voice.

"Don't try to run away from me again."

Then he walked away, I thought that he was going to leave me alone, and that it was all over, but I was wrong.

"Follow my steps, and don't let anyone know that you are following me," he said.

Though Bader walked and didn't look back, I found myself following him and walking behind him scared, confused, not knowing where he was taking me and what was waiting for me. Bader walked into a narrow street, and I walked behind him, tracing every step behind him like a thief. Deep inside me, I knew I was doing something wrong and I felt I was being watched like there were ghosts standing on my shoulders.

Then, we walked towards a motel. Bader stopped by the door waiting for me. He entered a motel, walked up the stairs, towards a corridor which led to a room by the end of it. Quietly, he unlocked the door of the room, after he made sure that no body was following him in the corridor.

The room was tiny. Everything was tidy and clean as if no human was a guest in this room at all. Bader sat on a couch and he stared through the window in front of him without say anything and without moving an inch. I sat on the bed quietly, trying not to make a sound, trying not to disturb his powerful and scary silence or interrupt his thought process.

"Look from the window", Bader said.

His face was so close to the window, his nose touched the glass. Bader looked at me, and he waved with his hand to me to come closer to the window. I got up from the bed and walked with slow steps and stood next to him, copying his body language and looking from the window to the outside world.

"From this window, you can see the Museum of Seville," Bader said. "**Th**at which you call home. They call it Seville. Look carefully, for when you see the Museum of Seville, know that you will see your future, and when you see the city of Seville, you will see home. Don't look at the Museum directly but look further away from it. Look and you will see what Seville means to you."

Then he spoke quietly, **"The** event is only a few days from today. Afterwards I will be standing behind this window, and you will be waiting for me at the door of the Museum. On the 28th of February, the eclipse of the moon will be complete. Everything will be dark. You will walk out of the Museum like a ghost, like a shadow." He paused and then said.

"But you will not be alone. You will be carrying the Tapestry with you."

Like a **Th**eatre rolling its curtains after a play, everything stopped; The time and the words, even the peace in this world. I felt as if a dark world resided, just like the darkness of the night. I felt that in my heart there was deep sadness not only for my beloved city Seville, and not only for myself, but a sadness that overruled the whole world.

"**Th**ere will be no light except the light of this street and this neighborhood. I will be here, and from this window, at 12:00 midnight, all electricity in the Museum will be cut off. By the time the police discover it you will be long gone with the Tapestry."

Then, I could swear I wished that I would leave this life without return: To run away to the furthest of faraway places, to disappear from existence. To become without existence, without a body, without a soul.

Thankless for the moment, I had a feeling that my love for Seville was turning into hatred. And Mira: I wished not to see her ever again in my life. Everything which was supposed to be under the mercy of fate, was dependent on my will. For if I want to, I can be a Moorish king and get out of the city with an Andalusian treasure or return back to whom I was: A mute moor.

Thoughts, endless thoughts. I spent the night with my eyes wide open. I remained twisting and turning in my bed between my thoughts, worries, and possibilities: endless possibilities. Like players in a match forced to strive, bare the hardships despite knowing they are going to be losers anyway. Like players playing the role of the heroes, and you playing the role of the victim and the loser.

Like a **th**ane, I laid on the couch, despite the agony. Maybe because I was fatigued, or because I was totally numb. Sleep finally took over and my eyes closed for a while. I looked through my half-shut eyelids and saw a beam of the sunlight shining from far away announcing the beginning of a new day.

Joseph: Light

يوسف

After the beautiful talk with Chihana, the youngster asked for permission to leave, so he could continue his journey which he started. The youngster told El-Khizr what Chihana told him.

"Prophet Joseph told his father: I see eleven planets and the sun, and the moon prostrating before me", El-Khizr said.

"My son, if you find the Nizam, don't go to the ends of the world to tell people of what you have found. Keep your secret inside of you. Don't disconcert yourself and lose your will. For people like the brothers of Joseph will envy you. What is envy but the worst of actions? Your brothers might throw you in the well, tell your father how the wolf has eaten you; this will make him cry."

"Would you leave what you worked on all your life? Would you let go of a love that you searched for all your life?"

"Don't run away from the winter, the rain, and from destiny. Maybe it was destined that the story of Joseph will be heard, and the truth revealed and learned. That Joseph's shirt was not painted with blood, but with paint."

"Nothing, my son, is created from nihility. Honesty and lies. Truth and untruth. The earth and the skies. The plants and the rain. Mercy and assault. Patience and aggression. Nothing is created from emptiness. And light? The universe is like a force of light that never switches off. Even if your light withers away, the light of the universe will live forever, for eternity, till the last line of the story, till the last word."

Chapter 10: Ra

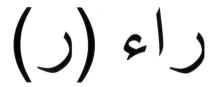

Roads were almost empty. I headed out before the sun rose, people were still sleeping. I was on my way to the Museum and despite my head being heavy. I started working on the new letters first thing. I made myself a cup of coffee. The steam coming from the coffee mug looked like clouds that shaped the way for a path that was already determined, a path that was already set.

Right then, I started working on the translations and I felt that there was a magical universal energy taking me to another world, as If I were not myself, and as if sadness that had overcome me was slowly fading away: like a solid heavy rock lifted off my chest. I felt as if the Museum was being lifted to the sky, I felt my body unlike my body and my heart different from the heart I got to live with all these years. I decided to finish the letter and go for a walk outside.

Rain was falling outside the Museum. I needed the rain to cleanse everything. For the rain to fall on my head and all over me, and to be at one with the sky. I preferred to enjoy being alone with my lonesome self, despite feeling that I was accompanied by a higher entity.

Rinse off the clutter; rain, rinse off the pain. Deeper, my sea of thoughts was sinking in the falling water puddles. Deep enough not to let me drown in a few centimeters of rain. I have had the feeling a few times; that I was as light as a feather, and that it was possible that I would fly, or for the wind to carry me and land me on a cloud, or on the top of a tree.

Remember Cosimo who escaped the world to live on top of a tree refusing to go down till the last day of his life? Some forms of madness are beautiful. A beauty that is not recognized by most people. A beauty to be free. A beauty that makes us refuse to conform. A madness that makes us change things and people around us, lest they understand those who surround us.

"Return back to the Museum," I told myself. Something told me to go back, a voice hidden inside. I decided to go back to the museum. I looked at my phone and I found a message from Mira which I have missed.

"Are you coming back to the Museum today?"

Run to her or run away from her? I decided to ignore the message for a few hours. What was scaring me on that day? I was absent-minded and decided to text my brother.

"Bader, I need to see you. I will be waiting for you after one hour in the lobby of the Motel."

Receiving no reply from him on my phone within the next hour, I decided to go to the Motel anyway.

Romanticized by all these events, I didn't know what was waiting for me there. I found my way easily like there was a map printed in my memory. I entered the Motel and walked towards the room. I opened the door of the room and went in. My brother was sitting in front of the window. He looked at me and smiled and then he hugged me tightly as if he was welcoming me after a long travel.

"I knew you were not going to let me down." He said.

He sat there puffing into the glass window in front of him.

"Do you know Rima"?

I was hoping that Bader hadn't spelled her name incorrectly. That he was looking for a Rima. No, I don't know any name that has a combination of M – I – R – A.

"Today I learned about the girl who is working at the Museum of Seville. She is responsible for the Tapestry," Bader said.

"Reverse the letters and keep them jumbled. Don't get them right, ever."

"What else do you know about her?" Bader asked.

"Remain ignorant of her, or anything that has to do with her. Leave her alone." Bader said.

I eyed him so that he may read the voice screaming inside of me. Other than the name, I don't know anything, I said to myself. I found a piece of paper and wrote "Nothing."

"Remember that if you fall in love with her, you'll be committing a big mistake. She could destroy what we have begun."

"What have we begun?" I wondered.

"Refrain from contacting me. Unless I tell you. Understand?" Bader said, then he added, "Stay away from her. That's your task. Unless you want to recall a number."

"A number?" I asked.

"Remember to recall the 4-digit number."

What Number? I asked again.

"The 4-digit number of the Chamber."

***

"Recreate memories to make something good of them."

"Reverse the time to create the first feeling of being born, or of not being born at all."

"Remember, and learn to memorize all details of your life, and the ticking of the clock in your remaining days."

Roaming in the city like a mad man, I thought I have gone crazy. I was going around in circles, and following my shadows feeling like there was no end to the trace. There I stood in the midst of the city of Seville, sounds of children playing far away, and the echoes of the buzz of the day was no more. I thought to myself, I thought a lot. I felt like I was a gladiator who had lost all his battles and his strengths, who had withered away after he had been expelled away from the world that he knew.

"Reminisce over the love for the city, which has become your shelter. Reminisce over the dreams gone and hopes of a great civilization lost from its warriors. A warrior or a worrier? I couldn't find the separating line between the two. I found them to be two faces of one coin flipped in the air. Whenever I thought I became a warrior, I would worry more, and fear everything and everyone: even myself."

"Remedy the wrong path which those people around you have taken. Remedy the misery, and the corruption of the world that has become what it is because of the people: Different names, different faces, same stories repeated over and over again."

"Religious fanatics, politicians, war mongers, kings, queens, poets, novelists, artists, doctors, engineers, and painters. You have to move on to correct the path of those who have come before you and pave the way for those who will come after you. But remember to smile and wake up with a hope that tomorrow will be better."

"Remember to smile", a voice said to me. I turned around to see where the voice was coming from.

Hud: Unity

"I am frightened, my Master. I am frightened, lost, and confused," the youngster said.

El-Khizr gazed towards the clouds and then said:

"The wind is blustering. Let us find a shelter to hide in, maybe we will build ourselves a tent or a shack."

"If the wind is strong it might blow it away," the youngster said.

"Don't be afraid of the gust my son, don't be like the nation of 'Ad. If you have built your home, the wind will not have mercy on you from wrath, unless you surrounded yourself with faith. Stand in the midst of the wind, and don't be timid."

"Know my son that when you are righteous you will have no fear. You alone will unite with the reality of existence. You will unite with your soul and with the sky. Don't be terrified, you were before in the void, and you will get back to it."

"You will be created once again. You will be born again. You will be united, resurrected, questioned, then you will live everlastingly. And you will be joyous. Unite with yourself. Unite with existence, your creator, your peace, and with yourself."

"Unite, for you are one in love. Even if the road was getting narrower, you are the soul that is renewed. Be humble in your prostration when you are a worshiper. Unite, but still don't be one-sided. Be a walking light amongst people, be an angel, and be a true friend."

"How is the person ever happy when he is lost in love? How is he ever happy who doesn't find his place in this world and who hasn't yet found love? How does he commit worship?" The youngster asked.

"How is he ever happy, my son, who wants all the wealth of the world? How does he sleep soundly at night and seek the long-lasting peace? How is he joyous who thinks that tomorrow he'll find certainty? Is he certain that his bed will remain warm when he lays his head down at night?"

"How is man ever happy? The one who thinks that joyfulness is a statue to be worshipped, like an end by itself. What do you take with you when you depart from this reality?"

"Beware my son, today, you wake up to remember your past, and tomorrow, you wake up to be a witness for the day which has passed. What do you remember when you are with the judge? What do you wish to become? Do you wish to go back to the best of childhood days? Or would you cry a lifetime of sadness, and your sins, and pains? What do you tell tomorrow when it comes? Would you refuse to shake hands with an old friend when the days have set you both apart? Or are you afraid to face death even before you are dead? For death is followed by life, and perdition is followed by an eternal end. Don't fear death but fear your dead heart. Your heart is your light, your pathway, your happiness, your life, and your worship."

"Would you want to find yourself a friend or a companion who will bring you any consolation? Be happy with all your senses, your breaths, and with every moment that passes by, even if the world closed down on you, and your companions have left you alone. For there must come mercy after punishment, and the hardships must ease, and after distress comes breeze. Fill your world with love, even if the journey extended, even if you were separated from the Nizam, for you must eventually meet her, for you are for her, and she is yours: time will not separate you, nor age, or even distress. For you are with her united like you are united with existence."

Chapter 11: Za

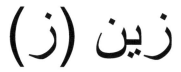

Zealous was the voice of the man with the white beard standing at a distance from me.

"Don't forget to smile Yassin," he said, as he moved closer to me. His face wasn't clear enough as he was hiding under the shade of the street lamp. He then turned away and left, leaving me struck.

A **Z**en-like feeling remained after he was gone. Like he was some kind of a time traveler, wearing his white cloak and white beard: Dressed in all white and snow.

Zoned out we were the next day in the Museum. Maybe I felt that I was betraying Mira because I was lying to her all the time, and the few countable hours we spent next to each other in the office were not enough. The minutes passed by as if they were hours. Sometimes brevity kills like a sharp pain cutting through you like a knife when you are around the person you adore the most. The walls of the museum have become mute and dreary.

"Shall we meet at 6:00 pm in the Museum when everyone leaves?

Please wait for me at the door of the chamber just in time and I will be there to open the door for you."

Saleh: Divine opening

Here, the youngster felt that his life was about to ease like the sky on a day where the heart is humbled, submitted to destiny and exhaustion. The youngster wondered, while he was walking with El-Khizr, which land he would settle in, and where the final destination would be.

After long days and weeks of walking, the youngster and El-Khizr saw a She-camel that was crossing the desert with pre-determined steps.

"I wonder where she is heading to," the youngster said in a lowered voice.

"Either follow her or let her guide you. You should be able to find an answer to your question, for if you wanted to ride on her hump, then she will be your servant, and if you want to follow her steps, she will be your guide."

"And what is there at the end of the road?" The youngster asked.

"Maybe the camel will guide you and lead you to what you are searching for."

The youngster followed the footsteps of the camel. The camel continued walking as if she was heading towards the mountain. Then she mysteriously disappeared and was no longer seen by the eye.

"Wait for her my son, for she must come back, and leave her hiding place, then you will know that you have received a sign to keep going."

"When the sky grants you a gift from within, don't deny and conceal it. When you see the sky calling you towards it, be enchanted by the calling, and don't let your pride lead you to your demise, like the story of Prophet Saleh and the Camel of God. When the people of Thamud, have asked him for a miracle from heaven: the calling was answered."

"Their camel came walking by from inside the mountain, but they have denied it although they have seen the miracle with their own eyes. Would you ask for water to drink and then spill it on the ground? Would you ask for food and leave it to rot? Would you ask for money and scatter it in the wind?"

"Would you ask for a calling, and deafen your ears so you don't hear a thing? If the Camel comes back, don't kill her like the people of Thamud. By killing it you will kill the voice of the truth and the voice of freedom within you. It's like you are killing the birds when they are chirping a melody of love, peace and freedom from captivity. It's like you kill the sky within you. Wait for the camel like you wait for the sky to open its doors for you."

"Do you know what the people of Saleh did to the camel?" asked El-Khizr.

The youngster replied with a question. "They slaughtered her?"

"They slaughtered her, and after three days, the shout came from the sky. The punishment came crawling down on them and the wrath."

"There she is," shouted the youngster. The camel showed up. She walked through the mist towards the youngster, but she was not alone: She was carrying a newborn human-baby on her back.

Chapter 12: Seen

Soon enough, everyone was already leaving the Museum. I was the only one who remained there besides the old pillars and ancient wooden doors. The doors of the museum would close at 6:00. I had to wait for Mira outside the chamber of Ibn Arabi till she came.

The **s**ky was turning orange, and the sun was setting. I waited for her there at the door. The chamber was like a throne sitting in the middle of the sky that leads to paradise. Mira was on time, perfectly punctual.

Stairs took us to the upper room. We entered the room and my head was memorizing the digits of the access code. The evening got quieter and calmer. The whiteness of the room became like the sun shining and glowing. White turning into yellow, and yellow turning into white. Mira sat next to me on the floor reading the letter as we were being taken away by the beauty of the Andalusian Tapestry. We enchanted each other, not knowing to which world this would lead us.

Secluded from the rest of the world by words. Maybe the best words are those that are never said, or maybe the best of times are those which pass by like lightning, quick, gone before the blink of an eye. You wish that those times would come back again. You wish to become whole like time: It does not diminish or increase, doesn't begin and doesn't go backwards. It doesn't end and doesn't have a determined place in existence.

Seeing Mira was like getting to know the meaning of existence, life, and love: She has become the metaphor of life for me. She was like the meaning of the heart becoming a heart, and the love becoming love.

Stop! What is time? What is existence? How do we feel existence and are we a part of it? Do we feel it because we are in it or because we are a part of it? In Seville, I became a part of the Museum – like I am an inseparable part of time – like I was an inseparable part of the whole existence.

Speaking of tomorrow, what do I tell Mira when she asks me about tomorrow? What do I tell her when her eyes ask me about the near future? Do I lie, turn away, and continue what I have started? Do I lie, wish for love to be lost, and for the best moments of life, the best of memories to be lost again?

To someone who has fallen in love, the hardest thing is to love and remain loyal.

But what is even harder is to grant that person the trust, to become like the mirror for them and them for you – a reflection for each other like two hearts sharing the sound of their own beats.

Shu'aib: *Heartly*

The youngster carried the newborn baby, may he find the baby's mother on this earth, so he can return it to her.

He looked at the newborn baby while it slept in his arms. "I haven't asked for a new soul, but for guidance," he said.

"Maybe with the renewal of the soul, you will find love, and may you be able to return the youngster to his mother, so you find blessing from a word from her, or maybe your life tomorrow will open its doors with a new beginning."

The evening began to fall and the sun had almost set. El-Khizr and the youngster found themselves standing at the doors of a village which they had not visited before.

The youngster roamed around the village and asked if anyone could lead him to the mother of the child, but none could.

"I heard there's a spice dealer in this village who will be able to be take us to the baby's mother. Let us visit him before the night falls."

After a few hours of searching, the youngster and his Master entered the dealer's shop, with the youngster still holding the baby in his arms. The spice dealer instantly recognized the new baby's smell.

"Are you looking for the baby's mother?" The spice dealer asked.

The youngster affirmed while still concealing his surprise.

"His mother no longer lives in our village, she has left since a few days ago when she learnt that her baby was gone."

"Can you take me to her?" The youngster asked.

"Follow her, before the morning comes, and before the light of a new day shines upon you." The youngster and El-Khizr went along tracing the steps of the mother of the child.

"My son! Go learn that the baby's mother is on the earth. When he, the baby, is close to his mother, his heart beats will recognize her. You, my son, are on your way to fulfill your covenant and your word. For if you succeed, you will be amongst those who fulfilled their promises, and if you fail, then you know you have tried. When you write your words, you want your words to reach out to the ends of the earth, and if you couldn't, then you know that you have at least learned. If you tried to reach glory, then you must have dreamt, believed, and prayed. And what if you didn't achieve glory after all? What if you weren't whom you wished to be, would you still be happy?"

"Be truthful to that, like Shu'aib called his people to serve the Divine. For the heart doesn't rest until it believes, and the heart doesn't feel joy until people's rights have been granted to them and justice prevailed. Are you better than your fellow man? How would you fool him? Do you prefer to be a king or a servant amongst your people? How do you see yourself in your own reflections? Would you die looking at your reflections in the water like Narcissus? Like Satan who let his arrogance kill him, and kill them?"

"Didn't I tell you I'm better than you? Didn't I tell you that I am made of fire, and you are made from clay? Didn't I tell you that I will survive until the last living person on earth?" These were the words of Satan.

"Don't be scared, my son, if you are amongst the truthful ones. Lift up your head to see yourself for yourself. You become your judge, and your witness. You will see yourself amongst your wrongdoings, and you will see yourself when you have saved yourself. It's never too late for repentance. You will find your destiny, and you will find what you are looking for."

"Look in front of you now, there's a woman sitting under a branch of a tree, her tears are falling down. Go to her, and give her the baby, so she may nurse him."

The youngster handed the mother her newborn baby. The mother thanked the youngster and praised him. She prayed for him and El-Khizr, and she took the baby to nurse him, but it was too late. The new born baby departed from this world.

The youngster was overcome with sadness. El-Khizr observed the youngster's sadness and told him a few words to try to cope with his sorrows.

"Don't be sad youngster. I wish you a prosperous long life. But I know that a smile from someone even if it came after a long-waited time is enough to replace your deep sorrows."

"You have drawn a smile on that Mother's face and wiped out the grief. You have made her joyous and brought her close to her child. This joy is enough. That smile was enough, for you will be rewarded for your deeds. Even if the fates have conspired against you, and you saw yourself far away, a lifetime or two, from your home: Away from the most beautiful moons, beautiful fates."

Chapter 13: Sheen

Shadows and dust. The hours passed by in the evening. I felt that the hours were like days, or months, or maybe years, that were eagerly awaited. A strange visitor fell from nowhere. I didn't invite him, and I wasn't waiting for him. A traveler from another time, to tell me what I was ignorant of, and what I failed to recognize.

Shall I admit I had seen him before, although I couldn't remember when or where?

"I know what you are planning to do. Don't step into that road. Don't lose the path of love and take the opposite road. For if you step into that road, you are vanished, forever."

He embraced me tightly in the dream, a deep embrace.

Shaken from what I saw, I looked up. The tiny window of the house was open. I woke up, but I didn't realize then what the nature of the vision was. Was it a dream or was it a reality? It felt so real. If it was a dream, why couldn't I speak and say something?

Shattered and scared, I decided to gather my strength and put my head on the pillow and sleep.

Maybe tomorrow I would completely forget the dream that I had.

Shameful, we wake up sometimes by our sins. And some other times we wake up, and we forget our dreams instantly, although we wish that we hadn't.

Power: Lot

"Go learn, my son, that a tyrant is in this village. If people of this village tried to live a different life, they will be eradicated."

"Why don't they face him with a fist of iron?" The youngster asked.

"The tyrant and his soldiers are powerful and mighty."

The youngster thought and said: "But they are not alone. For I am sure the people of this village are waiting for their promise to be fulfilled, for their freedom to be won."

"Do you see the village, my son, even if we are far away from it? Do you see the people of Lot in it? When they kicked Lot and his people from their village? If you see the people of Lot you will see the destiny of the village, and the fate of all villages. Don't be insistent on your one opinion and your one way of life. Don't be that leader, don't be that friend, don't be that King. Don't put yourself in a place where you love to be worshipped. Don't penalize people if they are different from you, and don't judge them. Befriend them, be with them, but don't follow their passions, for to each one of us adores his

own freedom, and to each his soul. You are like
life. Every day for you, there is a sun that rises.
Learn my son that you have no strength; only if
you are loving, then you will be joyous.

Part Three:

The Jet-Black Crow: The Body

"I am, a wisdom for the one who witnesses me. For I am the secret whose nature was fashioned when I was first created by my creator. For I am a rock, and from me, the spiritual meanings radiate."

--Ibn Arabi, The Discourse of the Jet-Black Crow, The Universal Tree and the Four Birds.

Chapter 14: Saad

صاد(ص)

Seam those random numbers together like an intricate thread of a dress. Could I spend my life in jail while my brother would live in an eternal faraway place celebrating his successful achievement?

Seville was everything to me, and I didn't want to go far away from it. But it was inevitable, and I had to be the villain to become the sole hero: I needed to take responsibility once and for all.

"My father is not in good health, so I will be late. I will come in the evening. If you finish working on the letter, you can go home, and maybe I will meet with you somewhere in the evening." Mira said.

So, I decided to spend my time in the Museum. I felt I needed time alone, and it was the perfect time to ponder and think about everything or maybe nothing.

Staring into the void, I felt connected with the story of the youngster, everything revolved around it like the earth revolves around the sun, and like the planets revolve around the solar orbits.

Stairs, oh the stairs above my head. The center was a few floors above me, and I felt I had the key to that universe. When everyone left the Museum, something splendid yet strange occurred to me. Something unexpected. When I decided to open the door of the chamber of Ibn Arabi, I found myself losing myself, as if I had forgotten about the world: The beauty of the Tapestry was splendid and magical.

Salute to the Tapestry. It was like a drawing engraved in memory - so real. But something was different: someone was standing there in front of me, again.

Send me back to my womb, send me to my tomb. My emotions were all a mess, a mix of contradictions. His embrace. I felt it. And in a flash, he was gone, again. He disappeared like he travelled to an eternal far away world. He disappeared leaving no trace, but another vague mystery.

Destiny: Ezra

While the youngster and El-Khizr were leaving the village, the youngster heard the calling of the woman.

"Come back young man, come close."

"I would like to thank you for everything you have done for me, and for your kindness. I would like to thank you for your bravery and strength. I wish that your days become like the moon shining, and that karma doesn't spare you. Even though I have lost my son, when I saw you, I felt that destiny had smiled back at me. I saw something in you: A youngster Nobel and kind."

The woman blessed him.

"You don't have to thank me for what I did." The youngster replied.

The woman continued. "You are also wise and generous. I have a feeling you have a long way ahead of you. You will learn a lot and will grow. In this pathway of life, you will find the moment. The memories will pass in front of you and you will know that you have lived a hundred years or more, having fully embraced every element of your story."

"Go now, go, and don't look back. May you and I meet again."

"By the way what's your name?" The youngster asked.

"My name is Malak."

The youngster headed back to continue his journey, thinking of what Malak had told him.

"My son! look around you. What do you see?'

"I see an open land."

The youngster looked and saw a donkey from a distance.

"When you see that donkey, remember the story of Ezra, who died for a hundred years, and then lived again.

He said, "Rather, you have remained one hundred years. Look at your food and your drink; it has not changed with time. And look at your donkey; and We will make you a sign for the people. And look at the bones [of this donkey] - how We raise them and then We cover them with flesh."

Proceed with your journey towards destiny. If you lose faith, you will slip and fall, and you will cry all your days, and your long waiting, your dreams, and wishes will be for nothing."

Chapter 15: Daad

She felt dead on her deathbed when she uttered these words to -herself: "Maybe he'll remember, maybe he'll remember that one day I was his only daughter, maybe he will remember the past one day, and remember me."

"**D**ear Mira," My letter began with this. But as I looked down, and there was no longer a pen or paper. There was the road ahead of us. Winter time was not over yet, but there was a hope that spring would be coming our way soon. There were no passersby, but we had decided to walk the walk baring it all.

Drifted from her story, we rested on a bench in the park. It seemed that both of us had been separated away from the other, both body and soul. I thought of the bearded fellow who showed up in the Museum. I thought of the madness, and I wondered: Would I believe someone if they told me that story in the first place? Was the old man weaved from my imagination? If it was so, how did I feel his embrace and why can I still feel him as if he was still with me?

"Maybe he still remembers his only daughter."

Mira said these words when she looked me in the eye.

"Maybe he still remembers."

Drowned in tears. She teared up while she was saying those words. I came close to look in her eyes, noses touching, lips touching trying to tell her that I feel every word she's saying.

"After all these years, my father doesn't remember it. He doesn't remember the past."

Do or Don't. Hold on to the memories or don't. Soon, they will become part of our present and our future. Soon, we will carry our memories with us when we leave this world. But how will we carry them when the body is not the same body, and the spirit is not the same spirit?

Displays like an exhibition that shows drawings we select and those which we don't. One day we see our memories in front of us like a cinematic film that will narrate all the events that passed and we experienced. Which of these memories would be recorded, which of them would remain, and which of them would wither away like the wind?

"I don't know how I will meet him again. It is so painful." Mira said.

"Every time the rendezvous is renewed when you meet your loved one it is as if you are meeting them for the first time. I will meet him like I was born all over again." She said.

And then she went on saying.

"I will, as if everything is fresh and new like the beginning of spring. I will meet him if he didn't remember me, even if he didn't speak to me". Mira paused.

"Come with me," she said, "I would like to show you something."

Jesus: prophecy

عيسى

The youngster continued his Journey towards his destiny. "Do you remember the day before you were born? When all you did was swim, sleep and weep?"

The youngster and El-Khizr rested under a shade of a tree.

"You were there under the shade. Half-light, not complete."

El-Khizr gazed towards the sun.

"Look for the light when you tread on this earth. Make your light luminate the darkness of the night."

El-Khizr then drew a line on the ground.

"Look here", he said.

"Could you talk when you were three days old, like the prophet Jesus? Be thankful for the Divine who gave you the ability to talk, the will to walk. My son, even if the sky doesn't rain on you yet, even if all that surrounds you is the barren desert don't give in."

"For you don't know when a tree will grow to make the desert an oasis, like the drops of water in the morning dew on your window. It'll wake you up one day, and you will know that you have lived for a legacy, like a prophecy. Like your existence is, like your life is. You are in this universe, and the universe is in you."

Chapter 16: Toh

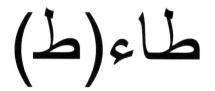

Time passed while Mira drove. I saw my reflection in the window. The car stopped, and we stepped out. The place was strange, a few closed shops, and a one isolated shop. A bird's shop, with a roof top.

Thrown in wonder and in some kind of amusement. Mira took a key from her pocket and opened the door.

"This used to be my father's bird shop," She said as we walked in, and then continued.

"I grew up here, while my dad grew old here. Birds, birds, he would spend all his time here. And now look at this place…"

To fly or not to fly? That was the question. Birds in a cage are like locked up queens, we love to lock up our queens and look at them. Maybe for the fear that if they fly, we will lose them, they will no longer be there to enchant us and amuse us.

Tossed in the middle of the sky like a bird with clipped wings, I passed by the cages. It felt like each one of these cages had its own love story. Like each cage was a city, had its own adventure, and its own world. I wanted to walk outside to get some fresh air, but her voice stopped me.

"Tomorrow we'll be free like these birds."

"Today." I said, while looking her in the eye. Mira took my hand. I felt my body so light like a feather. She was indeed the most beautiful creature on earth. Her eyes were like the full moon. Her face kindled with a peaceful glow. She had the most perfect scent, and her body and mine matched like the palms of the hands.

"Teach me how to love." Mira kissed me as she said those words.

Everything stopped turning and then the world started spinning with endless speed like two planets meeting at the center of a wide universe reaching out for eternity.

While we were going back to the Museum, I heard Mira's beautiful voice again.

"Will you promise me something?" She said. "Promise me."

She was quiet for a while.

"Promise me that you will never forget this moment, this touch, and this kiss."

To express how much, I have loved you? There was no end to this.

Solomon: Mercy

"Today, we walk, and we remember the mercy of the Divine, and the reoccurring mercies and the rain. Mercy is to walk on your feet, and to roam the earth. Mercy is to witness the world with your own eyes, and the flowers bloom."

"My son, the Divine has granted Solomon a throne that was not given to any of mankind before. He was able to talk to Djinn. In a blink of an eye, they could get him the throne of Sheba, hear the ants talk and understand the signing of the birds, and the words of the ants."

"If you had mercy on people, and they had mercy on you, peace will fall around you. If you kept the seal of the sky, and you grew to become a merciful father, and a merciful husband, you will live as if you have owned the throne of Solomon."

"Even if you owned all the wealth in the world, would you still be happy? Would anyone cry over a king the day he dies? What about a poor fellow? Don't be scared my son, if you didn't get the throne of Sheba in a blink of an eye - even if you were not Solomon."

The rain started pouring down heavily on the youngster and the Khizr.

"Where do we hide away?" asked the youngster.

"There's a Bedouin tent nearby. There we can find protection underneath it."

Chapter 17: Thoh

Those who love, and those who keep their promises: It was the distance between the earth the sky.

Through all of this, I promise you not to forget. I opened my eyes, and it seemed that we fell asleep on the floor. We haven't left the space which we were cuddled in. We were intertwined like a ring around the finger.

Though I promised her not to forget, I needed to lie to her. Goodbyes? Another story laid underneath like an ocean of water running underneath us.

Other, with each other.

Promises that death will not be our last resort felt like they were in vain. Promises that life tomorrow won't make us strangers or interns of love – and life.

Throw us life in each other's arms forever, but don't spare us. Don't make us like the birds in the bird shop: Sad, caged, and staged, living a lonely existence of life.

That which I call luck, and that which I call a strange coincidence. A coincidence to meet

Mira at this time: One coincidence like the strangest contradictions in the universe.

Then, there's the coincidence to meet the white bearded fellow in the Museum.

Think he was a guarding angel? Did he come to tell me that he's here, watching everything that happens, day and night: like Rakib and Atid; the two angels, sitting on our shoulders recording every bit of good and wrong doing.

The day passed by and I hadn't heard anything from my brother. The evening of the next day when I remembered him was like I had brought him back to life. I received a message from him on my phone. He has asked me to meet him outside the Museum. He pulled me by my shirt and dragged me inside the building where no one can see us.

"Say something. What's wrong with you?" I was going to say to him.

"Speak." Bader told me.

"Have you gone mad? Did you lose your mind?"

Thwarted by his voice. Everything turned black. I saw everything like it was upside down, as if I had fallen down on the ground. After I had gathered my strengths, I knew that Bader had punched me. His voice was muffled as if it was coming from afar. It echoed like my head was underwater.

"Didn't I tell you, not to try to fall in love with this girl? You're really dumb," he told me.

Thank you, brother, again. For the first time in my life because of you, I knew that I was no longer scared, that I didn't care if I lived or died as your punch had awaken me from a deep sleep: extended.

This next punch I took like a brave warrior. And the one after that. I stood up on my feet, and I found myself punching back at Bader.
Everything seemed to move at a very high speed. I couldn't see clearly. Suddenly everything slowed down until I gradually reached a full stop.

Thoughts, thoughts. Thoughts that mattered and those which didn't. All the voices vanished gradually, and everything faded away slowly.

David: Existence

داوود

There again, the youngster found himself in a place with someone whom he hadn't met before.

The Bedouin man welcomed them. His brevity overruled. He spent the night protecting his tent, his eyes wide awake.

In the middle of the night, the youngster heard sounds of quarrels outside the tent. When he looked outside, he saw an army of men. The Bedouin man fought with honor and pride.

The youngster looked outside as his fear was taking him bit by bit. The silence prevailed with only the sounds of swords hitting and the sounds of collapsing bodies. The sounds faded out. The Bedouin stood there frozen in his place, then looked over at the youngster and El-Khizr. He then took a deep breath and went back inside.

When the youngster and El-Khizr went back to the tent, El-Khizr looked at the youngster and said:

"Know my son, that if you were like David you could be fighting an army of men. You could be fighting Goliath. How do you win? When you are like David, the universe will be on your side, even if you were weak, and unexperienced in the battlefield. Be strong and stand still, and then even if you felt weak, you could become like David; you could become David."

Chapter 18: Ayn

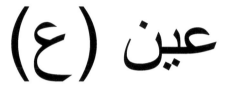

Ayn. The word "Ayn" in Arabic means an eye. It's also the 18th letter of the Arabic alphabet. Our eyes are two, one can still see with one eye, but one must see with two eyes to see clearly and sharply with full depth.

And there I was again. I woke up and my body felt heavy, like it was not my body. I was collecting all the parts like a jumbled puzzle. I decided to walk back home although it was a long way home. My face was still bleeding. Obviously, I was still alive but everything in my body felt so numb.

"Why didn't Bader kill me?" I thought to myself. "Was it because I am his brother or because he needed me?

I felt lots of pain, but also a sense of freedom: I felt fearless as I was walking back. It was the best time I spent with myself. I crossed over a pedestrian bridge. It was floating over the water, and I wasn't scared to look down, or even fall. I felt I was united with myself once and for all.

I arrived at the doorstep of my apartment when it was almost midnight. I must have wandered for a while, and lost track of time. At my doorstep again, I saw Mira sitting there waiting for me. When she saw me, she cried: I smiled a lot when I saw her. I kneeled down close to her feet - I collapsed.

I can't describe how serene I felt that night, despite the pain. The night was beautiful, as if it was repeating itself and Mira would take me, and I would live in her arms in the most precious silence and elevated beauty.

Astonished by my mess, Mira placed her hands on my head. It felt as if she was reading me verses from the Holy Quran. Verses from the chapter of the Merciful. I felt as if those verses were engraved on her hands.

"I feel as if you are like a child in my arms." Mira said. "I will protect you, I will take care of you. Please don't die, please stay."

I always wished to be like a child stripped of my wounds. Is there love without wounds? Is there life without hope that we can live tomorrow with joy? I wondered.

Mira went on to say.

"Is there life after death?" And then she looked far away and paused.

"If it was like that, I want to live it with you. Will it be forever? Will you be with me in it?"

Mira's words were strange. She'd never talked about the afterlife before.

"I never believed in life after death before."

Was this a question or a confession?

She went on to say, "I think there's a war happening inside of me. Something eager for truth. Is it love? Is it searching the meaning of love? How do I get a hold of it? It is untouchable, but I can feel it, and I don't know how to explain it."

After a few seconds, she continued, "I didn't ask you what happened to you, but I hope that you are alright. I am worried about you, and I don't want to lose you. Please tell me that you will be okay…"

Await the day when I will tell you everything. One day, I will tell you the story, but I hope that if I died, that love would stay strong between us: I hope that we won't go as far as the distance between the heart from the heart or the distance between the vein and the vein.

Again, we decided to remain close to each other like two eyes. Our eyes are two, one can still see with one eye, but still one must see with two eyes to see clearly and sharply; with full depth.

Away. Our ship sailed away. Even if it drowned, it is better to drown together. If we decided to live, I wish we would live together, even if we lived for moments. For that is better than eternal life separated.

Jonah: Breath

يونس

After a long walk, the youngster found himself standing in front of the sea.

El-Khizr walked closer to the youngster, then he looked towards the sun which was setting in the horizon:

"Appreciate every breath intake, for maybe one day you will find yourself drowning in the water. Look one more time, and see yourself drowning, see yourself living inside the whale's belly – like Jonah."

"Breathe deep till you transform into every breath you take. Till every breath makes sense. Breathe in front of difficulties and hardships. Breathe to forget your worries and sorrow."

"Breathe deeply for when you are dead, you come back to the belly of the whale. You will remain in it for three days and three nights, a miracle, like that of Jonah, for as Jonah was in the heart of the whale for three days and three nights, so shall the son of man be. And when you come back, would you come back to earth? Would you come back to the sky? Would you come back to the dream of eternity?"

"Breathe, let every breath draw your own path, and pave the way for you."

El-Khizr paused, and then continued looking ahead of him in the distance:

"Look ahead, there is a ship sailing towards us. We could sail with it, or let it sail without us. If we do, will cross the sea and we will arrive to the other side."

"What's on the other side?" The youngster asked.

"On the other side is a world where we all breathe the same air. A world without borders, without limits, where we all share the same land, the same sea, and the same sky..."

El-Khizr was silent for a few seconds. His silence, that of sadness, watching the shoreline as the ship continued heading their way.

Chapter 19: Ghayn

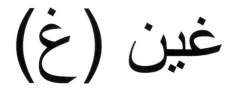

Gone were the days.

Gazing through the corridor towards Mira's office, I saw a man exiting her office. Who was he? He passed by me, as if I was a ghost. The next moments, I could tell that Mira felt anxious and scared. I walked into her office with hesitant steps. As soon as she saw me, she picked up a piece of paper and started scribbling some words on it, hands shaking. **There was only** the sound of the scribbling pen on the paper. "What was she writing?" I wondered.

She walked out of the office and left a paper on my desk. I read it. Couldn't she have said those words straight to my face?

I was taken aback by her unexpected behavior. She stormed out of the door. She didn't even look back or even look at me. Was it the end? I tried to follow her, I took one step forward, but something held me back. I stayed in my place by the door.

Grounded to earth. I decided to remain in my place, keep myself busy. "Was this day the last day I will see Mira? Will she be coming back, ever?

Overwhelmed by a stream of thoughts. I found myself in front of the garden of al Cazar Palace, in front of the small water fountain, like I was transported there.

The door was still open. I went in.

The greatness of the beautifully designed arcs struck me. The rooms spread across on the top floor. If I were a king, would Al-Andalus have stayed great like it once was? Would Mira be the queen and share all my victories and defeats with me? Then I thought that Mira was like Shahrazad, telling me a story every night, a cliff hanger every night for 1,001 nights: trying to save herself from myself.

Glassed was the water, like a mirror. I looked deeply into the reflections of the water. For a moment, I thought that I was Narcissus looking at himself several times every day. But the Narcissus in the water was not me and I wasn't him. He was someone else. The reflections on the water changed slowly from one face to another. It was the old man with the white beard again.

"Why did you let Mira go?"

This time I felt that he was the bearer and keeper of all secrets.

Then he went on to say:

"Go to her. She wants you to come to her."

Something inside me was telling me that I knew where I was going to find her. In my pocket, I kept the last letter which I had translated for her, in case this meeting was going to be our last.

Guided by my instinct, my footsteps lead me to where she was – the bird shop. The door of the shop was partly open, and I walked in slowly. Mira was sitting on a chair, an old wooden chair. I walked closer to her with slow steps. I put my hand on her shoulders. Mira refused to look me in the eye. I could smell her tears.

"What are you doing here? Please go away. I don't want to see you ever again. Go away," Mira said to me with a bitter voice.

In Grief, I didn't know what to say. I also didn't want to run away or go far. I wanted to stay. Putting my hands on her shoulders and smelling her scent.

"Do you know that man who was in my office?"

Mira stood up so that we were at eye level with each other.

"He is the secret police," she said.

And then she asked me: "The whole city is turned upside down looking for him, did you know that?"

Her grip on my hand was really tight. Mira moved closer to me until her face was so close to mine, I could feel her warm sweet breath.

"Did you lie to me? Swear to me, promise me that you have nothing to do with this…"

Struggling to prevent herself from crying, Mira held herself together. I knew after she said that my days with Mira were counted. It was like a dream that was fading away in a flash of light.

God! I thought as I was standing in the abandoned shop. The truth is difficult and sometimes sudden, like death, which comes like a storm: we don't know when it'll snatch us away.

Grazed by all of his sudden unalarming coincidences like a passing bullet. Mira left the shop and left me there standing among the empty abandoned cages.

Job: The unseen

أيوب

Sailing in the sea on the floating on water.

"My son, on this ship are people who suffered trauma. Look at their faces, what do you see? And into their eyes, tell me what you see?"

"I see some sadness, but I also see worry." The youngster replied.

The youngster walked closer to a middle-aged man, who was sitting on the deck looking far away in the distance.

Traumatized. Trying to trace the stolen goods. The middle-aged man, and his people were on their way to start their life anew; may they find new means of living.

"Patience." El-Khizr told the youngster.

"My son, not every awaiting is blessed, and not every waiting will bring a definite good. My son be patient if you could, like the patience of Job. You, my son, don't know the unknown, for some doubt is ignorance, and ignorance could be a bliss. Would you work hard certain to get the answer you are looking for? When does the unseen becomes seen, the unknown becomes known, the uninformed becomes informed?

When will the desert bring water, and when will the earth grow new seeds?"

"Know my son, that one day, you could become a learned man. Only when admit you are not, and all the knowledge which you think you have; is like one grain of sand."

Chapter 20: Fa

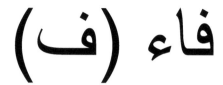

Fast forward. The silence lasted for only a few minutes. When I stepped outside of the bird shop, Mira was still standing outside.

"I want you to disappear forever. I'm giving you a chance to redeem yourself."

Fearsome, I just realized that I became an outlaw. How did I …?

"We are no longer meeting after the 28th of February. Please disappear from my existence, please..."

Fallacy, this whole thing is. How did the love story end even before it began? How did everything lead towards a dead end?

"I think I have loved you, but I was stupid. I made a big mistake. How could I have trusted you when I have never heard your voice?"

"Fool, you are a fool Mira. Do you think that love lives only through spoken words?" I asked her.

"Please forget everything. Go back to the basement, hand me the rest of the letters, and then go. Disappear." Mira shouted, before she cried.

Fallen. I fell into the basement like there was a hole in the ground. Mira refused to look me in the eye, not even for the last time. She didn't give me a chance to prove to her that I was honest: Loyal to our present and future together, I just needed a chance to tell my story.

That night, I was lonely. I felt I needed a companion. I went back to the Cazar palace, so that maybe I would see the old man with the white beard again. The door was closed shut at night. Of course, what was I thinking? I waited till the morning sun rise for the palace to open its doors.

***

Awaken by the beams of sunlight. Nobody came. I even felt that the old man had abandoned me. I had to go back to the Museum, but I didn't want to see Mira. I wanted to find a way to send her the letters without seeing her.

Flamed by the heat of sunlight at day and my feelings, I thought I would go to the motel room. There, I could write quietly, and no one would disturb me. There, I could still feel close to the Museum. I would feel like I was Mira's guarding angel. There, I would be far, but still near: Feeling her and counting the days looking for an end or making a wish that would make me vanish from existence instead.

John: Divine Majesty

يوحنا

The youngster excused himself so that he and El-Khizr could proceed with their journey. The ship reached the shore. The youngster felt that he was urged to continue his journey, and not be tempted by the invitation to stay.

The youngster apologized and continued on his way. On his way, the youngster heard the news that the people's goods have been returned to them.

On the way, the youngster told El-Khizr:
"Now I realize your words, my master."
"About patience?" El-Khizr asked. "Or about the unknown?"
"About both," the youngster replied.
"It's a mercy and compassion from the Divine, he grants them to whomever he wishes: To whomever was beneficent to his parents, to whom wasn't a mighty tyrant, to whom was compassionate and tender."
"My son, you can learn from the wisdom given to you, and from the stories of life – and people."

The youngster decided to keep his words to himself this time, and to continue thinking and meditating, hoping that soon, he could find the answers to his questions and find his love: His Nizam.

Part 4:
The Strange Anqaa'
"Phoenix": Dust

I am the one who has no existent entity.
I am the strange one, they call me, and the
door of my existence is sealed.
I grant everyone their secrets, and the
straight path stretches on and on.

*--Ibn Arabi, The Discourse of the Phoenix, The
Universal Tree and the four birds.*

Chapter 21: Qaf

قاف (ق)

Quietly, Mira sat in her tiny apartment. All the lights were dimmed. She sat there alone in front of her computer. She tried to write a letter to her father, but she couldn't express the words which she wanted to say. As she attempted to write a letter to her father, she typed a few words then she stopped. She picked up letters she had written to her father, and the words of Ibn Arabi. After a long pause, Mira looked at the piles of papers again and threw them in the air. The papers scattered everywhere, in slow motion. They fell down slowly like the snow would fall on a snowy day. She watched the papers as they fell down.

Quickly, Mira was bedazzled. She was trying to convince herself that she was sending letters to her father, but she was only hoping that her messages would reach him.

Quarrelling, Mira felt only pain and the agony. "How would he ever read my letters without remembrance?" Mira was delusional, she worked hard convincing herself that all her attempts to bring back her father's memories back were possible.

In a **Q**uest for unraveling more secrets, Mira rifled through the papers of Ibn Arabi's letters. She discovered words on the side written in Yassin's handwriting:

This is when the white bearded man showed up to me.

The **Q**ueer discovery made her ponder the thoughts, attempting to text Yassin at first. She couldn't wait. She left the apartment in a rush to meet Yassin, not minding the strife that was going on between the two.

Zachariah: Possession

"My son, would I guide you to a good deed?"

The youngster asked, "What is it my master?"

"Look far away, behind those fences, and tell me; what do you see?"

The youngster looked away and then replied:

"I see a high-rise wall."

"Behind the wall is a house."

El-Khizr rushed to destroy the wall with an axe.

"What are you doing?" The youngster shouted.

"Okay, that's it." the youngster said.

The youngster realized that he had crossed the line and raised his voice at his Master.

"My sincere apologies my master, I didn't mean to be rude. I am exhausted, and I can't go on any longer."

"Then go back to where you came from," El-Khizr said.

El-Khizr went silent, and then he said.

"Do you think that you can find your way alone?"

The youngster tried to conceal his feelings. He felt like it was not time to part ways with his master yet, for he still had a lot he wanted to learn.

"But now, since it is a goodbye, I would like to tell you things that were out of your possession."

"Think before you decide to go, before we part ways. Think of Zakaria, whom the Divine has granted righteous offspring after old age."

"Think of the wisdom of the teacher, of everything which have preceded. Think of everything you encountered, and go in your own way, but don't look back. Do you think you will still be yourself when your hair turns white and grey?

"Think, my son, of what came before you, and what's next. Think of what you possess and what you don't. And now, peace unto you my son, until we meet again and until our paths may cross."

Chapter 22: Kaf

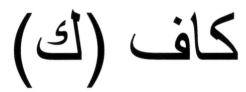

Keen to live a few moments of peace, I sat in the Motel room. The door of the room opened, and my brother came in with an embrace and a deep smile. Did he forget how he brutally beat me up?

"I am happy that you've got your reasoning back," he said.

"We don't have a lot of time left. We have to move fast. The city is turned upside down, and we don't want to be captured."

"We?"

"If we succeed, then we'll succeed. If we fail, we will have nothing to lose. If the mission fails, let it fail. I don't care. I will burn the place to the ground."

I thought that Bader could see the fear clearly.

"You are a hero, Yassin. Everybody will remember you as a hero. I love you Brother."

Karma comes back again. Who is the hero and who's the villain?

Heroism is a figment of our imagination which we have believed.

"When the time comes, run away and don't look behind you. I will be there."

Killers we are. I was trying to draw the line further between us. Every time I try to move away, I am drawn closer and closer to my end.

Elijah: Intimacy

ايليا

And when the youngster separated from El-Khizr, he felt an emptiness. Like he was saying goodbye to his best friend. The youngster stopped and regained his strength.

"I'm sorry," the youngster told his master.

"My son, our separation is surely happening. You alone are capable; you alone will decide your destiny and pave your own path. You have a long life ahead of you; you have tomorrow. Don't wait for someone to come and gift you your tomorrow like a plate of gold, or a cloth of silk."

"Strive in this life, and you will be. The path might change. Stay true to your vision and be yourself. Don't make your destiny a defined book, the `Divine is all knowing.

"Now let us part ways..."

Everything was quiet. The sky was quiet, and the atmosphere tranquilized.

"My son, between us is a good companionship."

"There is something burning in my heart. I feel It is not time for us to separate yet. May I become like you one day." The youngster said.

"Hereafter those years of drought and bareness, the sky will rain, after all the years of hunger, poverty, and drought. The hardships of the years will ease, and you will have affinity."

Chapter 23: Lam

Lost, l was sitting in my small balcony staring at the stars, at the sorrowed city when I heard a knock.

Listening to the knocks on the door, I wondered about the late-night visitor. When I opened the door, I saw a man. He was the man I saw in Mira's office. I tried to conceal my fears. He walked inside the room and sat on the couch.

"Look at me. We know what you and your brother are plotting for. You are under arrest..."

Then he paused.

But I won't do it!"

I felt relieved but at the same time worried.

"Unless you work with us."

He took out a paper and a pen and put them in front of me on the table.

"Life is too short."

He looked at his watch.

"I'll give you a few hours to make your mind..."

Do I tell him everything, or do I lie?

I felt the outcome was going to be the same: Either a lifetime sentence in prison or death.

***

Laying on the couch after, a few minutes later, there was another knock on the door. It was Mira.

Loved by her presence. Mira's curiosity didn't prevent her from jumping in with her question. Mira showed me the piece of paper which had the words I had scribbled.

"What did you mean by these words?" She asked.

It was hard to explain. Those words were like a word in-between millions of words lost, and others drowning deep inside the oceans.

Those were the words of the first meeting and last one. I knew what she was thinking just by looking into her eyes:

"I wish I could stay. I wish I could stay here like the beautiful fascinating spring. I wish I could stay in your arms, stay like the forever summer, like the dreams of childhood."

But she didn't say those words.

Like a mirror. Those were the words that I could see in her eyes. When the eyes start to flirt, the words lose their meaning.

"I love you."

Let's think of how a few seconds change us from strangers to lovers. Mira became the heart, and I became the beats: connected names like the sun and the moon, like the first kiss and the shivering of the body. Like child's first encounter with life, like the last breaths and the end of life.

133

Living those moments was astounding. I have never felt an embrace like Mira's embrace of me that night. I never experienced something as beautiful as those few hours: Like all of life itself, like they were the most precious moments I have lived – ever.

Luqman: Imamate

لقمان

El-Khizr said in a lowered voice to the youngster.

"Come with me, walk with me to the seashore, to the meeting place – where the two seas meet."

"I think I have seen this meeting place before" The youngster replied.

"Look there at the other side, you will see a small boat. There, you will find a woman, her name is Siwar. When you come back, I will be waiting for you at the junction of the sea."

The youngster walked a fairly long distance until he reached the meeting point. Siwar was awaiting him, sitting on the deck of the small boat. When the girl heard him approaching, she turned to him. Her face was angelic, as if it was an anomaly of light.

"Sit down young man," she said to him.

"Before you ask me anything, I have to ask you first. What brings you here?"

"I crossed all this distance looking for Nizam, looking for love. But I haven't found her yet."

"When I look into your eyes, I see wisdom, I see your destiny enlightened with greatness, I see you maybe a as a great king, a ruler, or an Imam for the people."

"How did you know all this? Do you foresee the future?" The youngster asked.

"When I look into your eyes, I see everything. When I look into your heart, I see everything before you. I see the wisdom of those who preceded you, as if you are Luqman giving people words of wisdom, as if you are a wise teacher, teaching man not to walk on this earth in insolence. You have ordered people charity, goodness, and prevented vice. I see you as patient, and enduring. I see you as someone with good faith, so listen to what I'm going to say."

"I know your destiny. I need a favor from you. When I finish my talk, turn around, and walk away from me, and don't look back. If you look back, you'll vanish, you'll burn and go back to the beginning."

"I am the phoenix. I am Siwar. I am the last pivot in the universe. I am your return to the starting point. I am the karma. I am life after death, and silence, and I am the noise."

"I am your phoenix. I am everything that endures hardships, and I am everything at ease. I am your life and your death, I am the water and the fire, and I am the earth and the sky."

"I am you. Now that you have come looking for the Nizam and for the impossible, looking for this eternal love, looking for dreams, let me tell

136

you a secret, let me tell you where you can find love, where you can find your Nizam. Nizam was everywhere, In every land, and every sea. Everywhere you looked she was there. Go back, go back to where you came from and where you have started, and where you took off at first, and then you will find her."

"Now, like I told you: don't look back. Don't ever look back. Or else, my beauty will burn you, my light will burn you."

Chapter 24: Meem

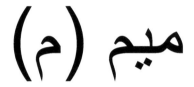

Mira: We begin with your name of four letters. M: My life I: Intertwined. R: Romantic like sunset warmth, like birds roaming the world. A: Adorable, and alluring.

Maybe you left the room now, and went back home, but you remain occupying the air in the space.

Might I have been distracted for a while. I needed to face reality again. The whiteness of the paper was becoming whiter, and the distance becoming farther.

Motel! That's all I could think of. I was exhausted. The noises woke me up with an adrenaline rush. I saw the police cars outside. The whole place was surrounded. The whole city was under surveillance. I had to run away, I had to disappear but nonetheless, I couldn't.

Mira. She was the only one able to grant me access to the Museum.

May God have mercy on the world. Everybody knew that I worked at the Museum. How would they have doubted a mute clerk anyway? A curse could be a bliss, sometimes.

Muzzled by Mira's question again. How do I tell Mira of that which I have no knowledge of? I thought for a few seconds and then I found myself there: in front of the Tapestry.

"Ibn Arabi," I thought to myself and then I smiled to Mira.

Moments before she left. I saw Mira sobbing. I saw her crying with agony. "He died," she said. She fell on my chest and cried more. And then she screamed: "He died; my dad died."

Imamate: Aaron

The youngster walked back. He found El-Khizr sitting in his place by the sea, unmoving.

"I am back," the youngster said.

"I knew you would be back," El-Khizr said.

"And that in your journey, you will be the Imam. You will be an Imam who will lead people and you will become someone of affluence. For you to become an Imam, you have to bypass a lot of obstacles, and you must become a learned man. But to be an Imam, you have to be fluent to defend affluence, like Haroon and Moses. Go back to the start, and look at Adam, look at the origins of speech.

My son! when you become a poet, and a savior for the oppressed, you will captivate hearts with your words. You will write the best of odes, and your words will save you from becoming a prisoner.

El-Khizr repeated those words: "I'm happy to tell you that you are here now. You are here now."

"Here where?" The youngster asked.

"Here, where the Nizam is."

"Where is she?" The youngster asked another question.

"Look here."

El-Khizr pointed at his heart.

"Look here, look here."

The youngster remembered his travels, like a nostalgic memory, that never existed. Like repentance, like trying to understand love, time, or destiny. Like light beams and the spirits, like the unknown, and the truth, and all of a sudden everything clicked for him: The youngster looked at the crashing sea waves, the rising sun, his eyes sparkled as if he came across a precious discovery.

Chapter 25: Noon

No one knew the end of this mystery. It was as if everything was coming to an end: fast. Even Mira was going to be gone for a few days for mourning.

Nevertheless, there I was in the Museum again, this time alone. How do I tell her to never come back to the Museum? There was no use in trying to explain anything. Silence was, for the first time, the antidote to fear.

Where is love formed and created? Does it grow in the depths of the earths, or in the deep oceans which are full of secrets? Is it created in the clouds, or in the depths of the skies?

Noon came.

Never knowing why, I decided to go to the Motel anyway. Maybe fear was driving me there. I went inside the motel, up the stairs, and into the room. My fearless brother was sitting in the room. His eyes sparkled, he didn't even smile. I wondered...

"There's a change in the plan" he said. "Everything is happening tonight. We are going to take the Tapestry tonight and disappear forever."

"No!" I wanted to scream. "No, I thought I had more time."

"No matter what happens, you wait for my signal. At exactly 12:00 midnight, when I send you a signal from my flashlight. If I don't send you a signal, you stay in." Bader said.

Night, on this night, felt especially dark. It was around 10:00 p.m. I felt nothing and everything at the same time. The seconds ticked, and the zero hour was approaching. The whole world flashed with thunder as I was looking from the window of the motel. "It'll be over in a few hours. Everything will be over."

"I'm at the Museum. I came to see you. Where are you?"

My phone beeped. I received a text from Mira. She was back.

"Mira, why did you come back?" I had hoped that my voice travelled to her crossing the walls of the Museum to tell her to go back and leave forever. Everything ended when Bader snatched the phone from me and crushed it under his feet.

Moses: Sublimity

موسى

Finally, the youngster felt that he came across a revelation. He felt like he was away from home, and now he's finally arrived. The sun while it was rising in the east. He looked at El-Khizr once again while he was still standing far away from him. For a second, it seemed it was the last time he would ever see El-Khizr.

It was like the sunrise was indicating a start of a new day and a new journey. The youngster walked towards El-Khizr, who turned to him and embraced him. The youngster felt that his bones were going to break. Moments later, the youngster felt a strange feeling inside of him: like death, like his soul was burning. The eyes of El-Khizr lit up like the sun. The youngster felt a relief that cleansed him of all his worries and pains.

"Now you know." El-Khizr said.

El-Khizr paused few moments, then he handed the youngster his cloak.

"Now that you have reached the seashore of peace, now that you have reached what you were looking for, you can continue your journey on your own, and answer the questions for yourself. Now that you can fly with your wings you shall travel. Now that you have received your cloak, you have become a complete human. Now that your journey is complete, go back and thank everyone who helped you. Remember you are never alone. This is where two seas meet, where the two lights meet, and where the two seas of knowledge meet: The eternal knowledge and the spiritual one."

"Now that you know, now that you have seen with your own eyes, go back. Go back to where you came from and meet once again with whom you loved. Now you are able, now you have something of the knowledge that will lead you along the way, that will make you a perfect human, that will help you finish your journey."

"Now, you own your body,
Now, you own your spirit,
Now, you own your soul,
Now you own your destiny."

El- Khizr started walking away with slow steps, and then disappeared from the youngster's eyesight. The youngster stood there alone.

Chapter 26: Ha

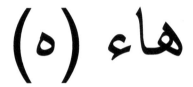 هاء (ه)

Have you lost your mind, Mira?

Hearts beating, I saw Mira standing at the door of the museum. She hugged me. It seems that Mira had plans that we die together in the Museum of Seville, so that maybe we can live together afterwards for eternity.

How do I tell her to stop time? If I told her, she and I will both die, and everything will be over. Police cars began to wail from afar. My brother was watching me with eyes that bore into my soul even from the Motel's window. I felt as if I was a dot in the universe, a dot that will create an explosion, then another explosion, and then another.

Her voice hollowed when she said my name. She was like a bird that shrank under the drops of rain. We went inside the museum. She didn't say much.

"I am here to see you one more time."

I sat on my desk while the rain was falling continuously. I sat there in the sad dark room, writing. My hands were shaking.

"So, is it the end?" She asked in a lowered voice. "This is where we end?" She asked me. Mira walked closer to the window and rolled the curtains down.

"Have you wondered, why I am back? I had to come back for you." Then she paused and looked at me. "To protect you from yourself," she said in a sad voice.

Heartbroken. I walked closer to her and looked into her teary eyes.

"Look outside, they all came for you. As soon as you write the last letter. Please do as I tell you to do."

Then she went on saying heart breaking words. Her final words:

"Can I tell you a something? This was the best month I have ever lived in my life."

My hands were shaking, my scribbles were not clear. I gave the piece of paper to Mira. She took it from me. She tore it into pieces, and with it, she tore my heart into a million pieces.

Here came the end. In a glimpse, the police stormed inside the museum. Everything ended in a few seconds. Mira was still standing there. Handcuffed in the police car, I looked one more time towards the museum.

Hollowed by the light of fire. It was like the sphere of the sun lighting up the darkness. Everything turned into silence, all the sounds were silenced, except the flames, flames, and flames, rising up in the dark night sky. The radio in the car crackled and announced the news.

147

Flames reflected on the window as I sat in the backseat handcuffed, looking at my reflection in the glass realizing that it was all over.

Khaled: Refuge

خَالِد

In the beginning of separation, there was nostalgia. The youngster thought of El-Khizr's words over and over again. Strangely, he didn't feel the agony of separation because the cloak made him feel as if El-Khizr had never left.

The youngster thought he should be heading east, then he thought of going west. After days and days of walking, the youngster found a tree, and decided to rest under its extended branches. Between confusion and amazement, the youngster felt that he was living in a world which was different from the world which he used to know.

A voice called onto him coming from the branches.

You are living now in the world of the Isthmus, you are living between the past and the present, you are living between existence and non-existence," The youngster looked up towards the branches.

"Look for your last refuge, and don't wait for me, for I am not coming back. You are now heading to eternity, you are now getting close to the last breath. In the Isthmus, your world will be different from the world you used to know, and your existence will be different from the existence which you know. In the Isthmus, you will unite with your soul, you will exit your world, and enter the world of the dream, to the world which exists between stillness and motion, which exists between inertia and perpetual motion. You are now a newly born child. Look around, you will see everything anew. Look around, you will see like you haven't seen before: You will see with your heart, not with your eyes. Look around you, you will see with your soul: The veil has been removed from in front of you, and your eyesight today is sharp. Nothing separates you from the truth, except a thin line, like the line between the sky and the earth. Can you see clearly now? Can you see what you couldn't see before? If you could see, then you must have seen the true vision."

The youngster felt light headed and felt a sudden dizziness. He felt like he was living outside of his body, like he was weightless, feeling numbness. All the voices slowly faded away, and the youngster transcended into another world.

Chapter 27: Wow

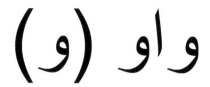

Where was she? Mira was gone, and so was I.

We got separated from our past. Snatched away. Every time I would go back in time, the memory of her would come back with the fever and the agony, like illness. How long have I been here? Ten years? Fifteen years? I stopped counting the days.

Sitting in the tiny prison cell as I was waiting for the unknown. I wished that nothing would change, and for everything to remain the way the way it is.

I was awakened again by a voice in the middle of the night. From the small tiny window that overlooked the street. I heard the voice of the white bearded man again.

"Don't lose hope, my son".

I peeked from the tiny window where I could see.

"There's still hope," the voice said again reassuring me.

The voice went on saying: "There is still hope for you, you are not dead yet. There's still hope, for you are still alive."

Then the voice continued:

"**W**hy don't you want to leave this place? Leave this place if you could, leave it and you will be good."

With his rhyming words, I wished I could ask him about Mira and what occurred to her. Did she die? Did she find someone to bury her pure blessed body in the soil? Does an angel like Mira die?

I sat there still banging my head with the walls, between a thought and the other, the sun was rising, setting, rising, and setting again and the days and days passing by and by.

Days later, my prison cell door was opened by a prison guard, and then an officer. He took me out my cell.

Into **w**hat looked like an investigation room. We sat there, silence. He took out a paper and placed it on the metal table.

"**W**rite"

"**W**rite?" I wrote.

"**W**rite," he said again.

"**W**rite what?" I wrote.

"**W**rite down everything, write your testimony, your story, if you desire your freedom."

Walls. Surrounded by walls. I sat in my prison cell writing everything down. Everything. I was only thinking of freedom and salvation.

I **w**rote it all down. That was my story.

I **w**rote it as it happened with me in all its details.

Mohammed: Singularity

محمد

The youngster woke up to the color of the blue clear sky above him, to the sound of birds chirping. He found himself sitting underneath a tree, staring towards the sky.

"Where am I?" The youngster asked.

"You are here now, you are here with us." A voice answered.

The youngster didn't know where the sound was coming form.

"Who are you?" The youngster asked.

"We are the four birds; do you remember us? You have passed by us in your long journey. You were blind. Your eyes were blindfolded, but now you can see."

The youngster looked up. The chirping faded out, and all he could hear was the bird's speech.

"I am the Jet-black crow. I am Yamama. I am the sand. We met in a foreign land, you held my hand, and in my house you stayed. I am your body; I am the world in which you recognize things. I am the extinction. I am the one who carried you, and who was with you. I am the one who protected you, who gave birth to you, and who made you die. I am the crow. In me, you have lived all this time, and in me, you died. You have seen me before, but you haven't recognized me. You thought that you were forever eternal through me. You thought that you would live in me. You thought that you were going to live forever. You thought that you were made out of nothingness, and that from darkness to darkness you would return. I am the crow. I am Yamama. I am the answer."

The crow went silent, and the youngster heard another voice calling onto him:

"I am the Royal Eagle. I am Chihana. I am the woman with the vision. Remember the old man and his daughter? I am the feeling. I am what no one contemplates. I am the soul. I am the sky. I am the air. I am the human being. I am your existence and all your promises. In me, you unite before and after existence. In me, the crow unites. Without me, the existence is a sea without water. Within me lies every secret, every cure, and every medicine. All the secrets of the universe and the keys of knowledge lives within me. I am the keys of the universal knowledge, from Adam to Mohammed. I am the key to eternity."

The youngster listened carefully to the Royal Eagle's words, then he heard another voice coming from the tree.

"You have seen me before too. You have recognized me before. I am the ringdove, I am Malak. I am your first encounter with life, you saved my child, although he died. In me, you grew, you learned, and in me, you became what you have become. In me, you learned your alphabets and realized that your existence in this life is mortal. In me, you thought deeply, and with me, you read and wrote. With me, you read your Quran, and with me, you found the names and the dreams. With me, you dream, and you see. I am the ringdove; I am the line that separates the earth from the sky. I am all the names which were given to Adam. I am love and life, death and survival. I am forgiveness and disobedience. I am the human shedding blood and doing good. I am the "Aleph" to the "Ya". I am your brain, your strength and weakness. I am your will and you're holding on. I am the lines on the back of your palm, I am the lines of your life, you draw me however way you want. I am the brain. I am the place between the soul and the spirit. I am the memories; you direct me however way you wish and desire."

"What about you?"

The youngster asked while he was looking at the top of the tree. The bird responded:

"I am the phoenix. I am Siwar. I am the beginning and the end. I am nothing and I am everything. I am the phoenix. I am the nothingness. I am what comes after death and beyond existence. I am your loved one. I am the rendezvous which you were seeking, and I am the last appointment. I am the phoenix. I am the crow, the ringdove, and the eagle. I am the remaining. I am the ocean of your secrets. I am the mirage. I am the last word, and the end of the trip. I am the 28 letters, and I am the voices. With me, you complete your story, and with me, you become complete. I am the meeting of the sky with the sea, the eternal meeting, the last of resorts, and the last of the ships. I am the phoenix. I am every meeting. Do you recognize me now?"

Afterwards came the silence, which lasted minutes. The youngster was still in surprise.

"You are complete now, and you have achieved the impossible. You are patient. You have learned and travelled across the earth. You alone can now finish your story, go and live your life."

The four birds spoke in one voice:

"And Nizam, which you were looking for, and still are, lives inside of you. She was and still does live inside of you. You searched for her, and you haven't found her, but she was always with you, she has always been. Although Nizam lives in your imagination. She is you, and you are her. No matter how long you have looked for her, you will never find her, unless you wanted to see her, unless you had the desire to meet with her, unless you have lived for her, and gave to her, and adored her, a pure adoration, a united adoration, an eternal adoration that is never renewed."

"It is in her that you live forever, and she lives inside you forever. With her, you die, and with her, you live, until she becomes your soul, your hometown, your ship, your words, your victories, your defeats, your sea, your sky, your heart, your travels and journeys, your beginning and your end."

Chapter 28: Ya

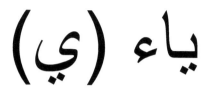

Yesterday Mira woke up. Next to her bed, she found a letter. She recognized the handwriting. It was Yassin's.

Yassin was back? She couldn't believe it. She started reading Yassin's letter:

You must be asking yourself lots of questions like I have asked myself over and over again. Today, I learned that you are still alive. All these years, I thought you were dead. At least, now I can sleep at night.

You wonder how life passes us by and if we ever got the chance to explain to the ones we love, the things we always wanted to say, would we dare to?

You wake up one day, feeling different, like a new person. You ask yourself: what has changed and what has made the difference? Instead of waking up with guilt, worry, and pain, you wake up feeling alive because you can still breathe.

Yassin, you might ask yourself, who is Yassin? I am but a normal person, a passerby, a traveler in time. You ask me if I smile when I remember you. I do. Every time I remember your name, I do. Every time I pass by the streets of Seville I remember. And smile. And every time I pass by the Museum of Seville, I do. I smile when I remember that sometime ago, not so long ago: we were one in love.

You ask me how is it that we never uttered words of love to each other? I wish I had the answer to that, but I surely know that I have loved you. Remember the piece of paper which you tore up the last time we met? I wish you had opened it then, but I guess we can't reverse destiny and rewind time. There were three words written on it: I am Innocent.

Yes, I was about to forget, the Tapestry. If you go to the garden of the Museum of Seville, you will find it buried there. The Tapestry, as you might have guessed, holds a universal secret, a secret and mystery that is similar to that of love.

You must believe me. I never meant to cause you any harm, and if we meet in this life or the next, I want you to know that you were my first love and my last.

Yassin, with love.

-- : --

And so, Yassin left, leaving behind him all the memories. He left like we never existed, like we never met, like we never were. Yassin left. Although his name started with the last letter of the alphabet, he was my genesis.

Isn't it strange that Yassin was mute, and that his letters started with the letter Aleph and ended with Ya'?

I spent the days looking at the Tapestry of "Ibn Arabi" and rereading the letters over and over again. In the buried box which had the Tapestry, I also found a silk cloak. I shivered when I picked it up.

Despite Yassin being mute, he was able to change something in me, and teach me the meaning of love and a million reasons for appreciating the gift of being in this world: birth, life, and death. The blessing to be able to love, and to be able to say that you love. The blessing to be able to be good, and to do good. The blessing to live in this world, and to be thankful for your existence and for the air you breathe every morning, for you know that a day might come where your journey will come to an end, but deep within your soul, you knew that you have lived that life you were grateful for – and that with words, you were able to bring something valuable to existence and change it for the better.

With these letters, I saw the world in a better way, although I have hoped every day that I

161

would see Yassin again – but it was enough when I would lay my head to sleep to see him standing in front of me with his smile, and his eyes which said a lot: and still do so every day.

Who is Yassin? Was he Ibn Arabi himself? Maybe he was a traveler through time trying to tell us something: The meaning of love, life, and existence. The only thing we can do is open our eyes and hearts and listen. Maybe this secret would one day be revealed and passed on to generations to come. Did it really matter? I am not sure. All that mattered was that he was a man I have loved – and maybe, just maybe, Ibn Arabi was here as well: Heart, body, and soul.

Printed in Great Britain
by Amazon